The Tanglewoods' Secret

Patricia St John

Revised by Mary Mills

Illustrated by Gary Rees

Scripture Union

© Patricia M. St. John 1948
First published 1948
This edition first published 1999, Reprinted 2002

,

Scripture Union, 207–209 Queensway, Bletchley,
Milton Keynes, MK2 2EB

Email: info@scriptureunion.org.uk
Website: www.scriptureunion.org.uk

ISBN 1 85999 267 6

Printed and bound in Great Britain by
Creative Print and Design (Wales) Ebbw Vale.

Scripture Union is an international Christian charity working with
churches in more than 130 countries, providing resources to bring
the good news about Jesus Christ to children, young people and
families and to encourage them to develop spiritually through the
Bible and prayer.

As well as our network of volunteers, staff and associates who run
holidays, church-based events and school Christian groups, we
produce a wide range of publications and support those who use
our resources through training programmes.

Contents

Titles by Patricia M. St. John

STAR OF LIGHT

TREASURES OF THE SNOW

THE TANGLEWOODS SECRET

RAINBOW GARDEN

THE SECRET OF THE FOURTH CANDLE

THE MYSTERY OF PHEASANT COTTAGE

For older readers:

NOTHING ELSE MATTERS

THE VICTOR

I NEEDED A NEIGHBOUR

For younger readers:

THE OTHER KITTEN

FRISKA MY FRIEND

Revised edition

It is over fifty years since the first editions of Patricia St John's *Treasures of the Snow* and *The Tanglewoods' Secret* were published and they have become classics of their time.

In these new editions of the books, Mary Mills has sensitively adapted the language of the books for a new generation of children, while preserving Patricia St John's superb skill as a storyteller.

References to money are pre-decimal currency: 1/- (one shilling) equals 5p. There were 12 old pence in a shilling and 20 shillings in a pound.

Chapter One

About ourselves

Philip and I lived with our Aunt Margaret in a white house on the side of a hill. It was a lovely home, with a garden and an orchard of apple trees. We slept in two attic bedrooms at the top of the house and had our doors open so we could shout across to each other. Philip's window looked out on the garden with the hills behind it, and it made me feel very safe. My window looked out over the countryside of Worcestershire, with the hills of Herefordshire in the distance, where I had never been. My view made me long for adventure.

I loved looking at the hills, and when Philip came to sit on my bed in the morning to listen to the first bird songs, or watch the sun rise, we used to make up stories about strange animals that lived on them.

Philip was a year and a half older than me, and I loved him more than anyone else on earth. He was gentle and thoughtful and once he had made up his mind about something, he wouldn't change it! He had always been my friend and protector, and we were never apart, except when we were at school. We were so different – Philip was a big, strong boy, with a round face and blue eyes. I was small and thin, with dark, untidy hair and a pointed chin. Philip was good and obedient but I was naughty and hated being told what to do. Aunt Margaret really loved Philip, but she shook her head sadly when she looked at me.

At the time of this story, we had been living with Aunt Margaret for five years. We had forgotten what Mum and Dad looked like. They lived and worked in India and they had sailed away when I was just four years old. Mum was going to come home, but the war had stopped her. I was worried that Mum wouldn't like me if she did come back, as Aunt Margaret kept telling me how disappointed she would be with me because I was so bad. In her letters, Mum sounded as if she loved me very much, but I thought that must be because she didn't know what I was like. I was sure she would like Philip much better than me because he was a good boy, and grown-ups always liked him. Philip would like Mum, too, because Philip likes everybody. I wanted Philip all to myself, so I tried not to think about Mum coming home. I didn't want to share him with anybody – not even our mother.

But Philip could remember her, and sometimes he talked to me about her. I always remember one evening, when I was about eight years old, I had been sent to bed without any tea, because I had been naughty. I was lying on my bed feeling hot and angry and very hungry, waiting for Philip to climb the stairs on his way to bed. As usual, he came straight into my room. He bent down and struggled to get something out of his sock. It was a sugar-bun which looked rather squashed, and it had lots of wool sticking to the sugar. Philip was very proud of it, as he had managed to get it into his sock, under the table, without Aunt Margaret seeing him. I ate it happily, while Philip sat on my pillow and put his arm round me.

"What else did you have for tea?" I asked, with my mouth full of bun.

"I'm afraid we had meat-balls," he replied, "but they were too squashy to put down my sock. They weren't very nice – you didn't miss much."

"It's very unkind of Aunt Margaret to send me to bed without my supper," I whined. "If Mum was here, she wouldn't be unkind to me like that."

"No, she wouldn't," agreed Philip. "But then, you see, you were really, really rude to Aunt Margaret, and you would never have been rude to Mum."

"How do you know? I might," I said.

"Oh no, you definitely wouldn't," said Philip. "There wouldn't be anything to be rude about. You're only rude when you're cross, and we were never cross with Mum. She was so happy and bright. If we were a bit naughty, she used to pick us up in her arms and tell us lovely stories – then we'd forget all about being naughty. I wish you could remember her, Ruth."

I was just about to ask Philip more about Mum,

but he suddenly hopped off my bed and dived across to his own room like a frightened rabbit. I heard Aunt Margaret's footsteps on the attic stairs.

She went into Philip's room and I heard her cross over to him and tuck him up. I heard him say, "Good-night, Auntie" in a breathless sort of voice. Then she came across and stood in the doorway of my room.

"Good-night, Ruth," she said.

If I had answered and said I was sorry, she would have come over and tucked me up, too; but I hated saying sorry, so I pretended to to be asleep, and gave a very loud snore. Of course, she didn't believe me.

"I'm sorry you are still in such a naughty temper," she said in a cold voice, then she turned away and went downstairs.

"Did she see you weren't undressed?" I whispered across to Philip.

"No," answered Philip. "I pulled the bedclothes round my neck. Good-night, Ruth."

"Good-night, Phil," I answered, and turned over towards the window and stared out into the darkness. I kept thinking about what Philip had said about Mum. Mum would have come across and kissed me, whether I was sorry or not, and then of course I would have really been sorry, and Mum and I would have looked out at the stars together. She would have told me stories. As I fell asleep, I could almost feel her arms around me, but in my dreams she ran away from me, and she and Philip went away together, and I was left behind.

Chapter Two

Holiday plans

This story begins two years after the night I told you about in Chapter One.

I was now nine and a half and Philip was nearly eleven. On the first day of the Easter holidays Philip came into my room in his pyjamas at half past six in the morning. He curled up on the end of my bed with a notebook and pencil in his hand. Together we leaned our elbows on the window-sill to watch the birds and to make plans.

Bird-watching was our great hobby that holiday. We had a notebook in which we recorded each different kind of bird we saw and everything we noticed about it – its song, its nest, its habits. Philip had made the book himself, and it was very neat. He did all the writing and I painted the eggs when we found them. Philip's work was exactly right but my drawings were not very good.

Philip longed for a camera so he could photograph the nests.

"If only I could take photos of them," he would say, over and over again. "I might be a great naturalist – my book might even be printed."

But the cheapest camera in the shop-windows cost pounds, and our money-box held exactly nine shillings and sixpence, even though we had been saving for weeks and weeks. We emptied the coins onto the bed and counted them once again, just in case we'd made a mistake the time before. But we hadn't. Philip sighed deeply.

"I shall nearly be going to boarding school by the time I get that camera," he said sadly. "I wish we could earn some money, Ruth."

We gazed out into the garden rather sadly, trying hard to think of a plan, but we couldn't think of anything we could do. It was April, and the first fruit trees were all covered in lacy white blossom. Yellow primroses and daffodils shone brightly in the sun.

All of a sudden I felt Philip's body go stiff beside me, and he half dived out of the window.

"Tree creeper – on the plum!" he hissed.

I leaned out beside him and we watched a neat brown bird running up the plum tree, tapping the bark for insects. Philip was alert now, noticing everything he could about the little bird until it spread its wings and disappeared. Then out came his notebook and for the next five minutes Philip was busily writing down everything he could remember about the tree creeper.

Then he looked up. "Ruth," he said eagerly, "we

must get to the woods early today and have plenty of time – and Ruth, I was thinking in bed last night, we should have a naturalists' headquarters. We should have a place where we could keep pencils and paper and tins of food, instead of always carrying them with us – because we shall go every day all the holidays. We must escape early before Aunt Margaret thinks of jobs we ought to do."

I nearly fell out of bed with excitement.

"Yes – we'll race through our holiday jobs – and I'll be as good as gold, so she'll hardly notice me, and she won't watch me, and when I've swept and dusted in the lounge I'll just slip out before she thinks of anything else. If she asks where we've been we'll say we've been getting wood – and we'll bring some back to make it true – but I don't see why we should have to work at all in our holidays! I know what I'll do – I'll dress quickly and go down now and help Aunt Margaret with breakfast to make her think how good I'm being!"

I was out of bed in a flash, and ten minutes later I was down in the kitchen with a clean apron on, and my hair neat and tidy.

"Can I help you, Aunt Margaret?" I asked politely. "I got up early in case you might need me."

My aunt looked very surprised as I was usually very late in the mornings.

"Thank you, Ruth," she answered pleasantly, hiding her surprise, "you can lay the table for me. I should be very glad."

Everything went smoothly. Philip and I ate our breakfast very fast and sat impatiently while Aunt Margaret and Uncle Peter slowly sipped their second cups of coffee, discussing the day ahead.

11

Then Uncle Peter went off to work and Aunt Margaret turned to us.

"And what plans have you two made?" she asked.

Philip had the answer all ready. "As soon as we've done our holiday jobs, we're going to get wood in the Cowleighs, Aunt Margaret," he replied, in his sweetest voice.

"Very well," my aunt answered, sounding a bit doubtful, "but you must remember I need your help in the mornings. Ruth is old enough to help in the house now; she can start with wiping up and doing the lounge, and then we'll see."

I could be quick when I liked, and I wiped up the breakfast things in a very short time. Then without saying anything more to my aunt, I seized the broom and duster and headed for the lounge. I flicked the dust off the shelves at high speed. I pushed the broom wildly round the edges of the room then lifted the carpet and swept the pile of dust under it, as I couldn't find the dust-pan. Then I tiptoed back to the kitchen, put the broom and duster back in the cupboard and ran out of the front door like a streak of lightning.

Out and free on an April morning, with the sun shining and the birds singing, and the lambs bleating! I tore round the back and pounced upon Philip all unexpectedly, nearly knocking him over; but he was quite used to me by now, so wasn't really alarmed.

"Finished already?" he enquired, rather surprised.

"Yes, haven't you?"

"No," he answered, "I've got to chop these sticks

into kindling wood. It will take ages."

"Oh!" I cried, "We can't wait! You've made quite enough of those silly bundles. No one will know we haven't chopped them all up if they can't see the rest. Quick – give those sticks to me!" And before Philip could say anything, I had thrown the rest of the sticks into the ditch and was kicking dead leaves over them. "And just think," I shouted, jumping up and down, "how quickly we shall find them when we are sent to get more!" – and with a final leap I was away across the orchard and out through the gap in the back hedge like a young rabbit, with Philip at my heels.

No one else knew about our gap in the hedge – it was our own special right of way. Aunt Margaret could see the gate from the kitchen window, and sometimes we didn't want anyone to know about our comings and goings. So we had found a gap, behind the hen-house, which was invisible to anyone else because it was covered by overhanging branches which we brushed aside. It led out into another meadow, which led to the road and in turn led to our dear woods.

Once in the road I danced and shouted like a young mad thing. It was sheer joy to be alive on such a morning. Philip followed more quietly, his eyes fixed on the hedges, now and then stopping to listen or to watch. I did not wait for him; I felt as if Spring had got into my feet. I think I scared away most of the birds before Philip came anywhere near them.

I jumped over the gate that led through the meadow and stood still for a minute, watching the mother sheep with their joyful, long-legged lambs, leaping, like me, among the daisies. And as I watched, one of the lambs with a smudged nose and black socks suddenly saw me and came rushing towards me, giving little bleats of welcome. I bent down and held out my arms; he ran straight into them, and started licking my face with his eager, warm tongue.

"Philip!" I cried. "Phil – look what's happening!"

Philip was beside me by this time, and together we knelt in the grass while the little lamb prodded us, licked us, and leapt from one lap to another. As we played, an old shepherd came and leaned over the gate, smiling at us.

"That's the little orphan," he explained. "He's bottle fed, and he's not afraid of anyone. The other sheep push him away, so off he goes on his own. He's always in trouble, the little rascal!"

The lamb at this moment leaped from my knee and ran to the gate; the old man stooped and picked it up.

"He knows my voice all right, don't he?" he remarked, smiling. Then, tucking it inside his coat, he turned away towards the farm.

"That's a new shepherd," I said to Philip. "I've never seen him before."

"I have," answered Philip. "He's over from Cradley for the lambing season. Come on, Ruth! we're wasting time!"

He jumped up, and we raced across the open meadow with the wind blowing my plaits out behind me; then over a stile, and we were standing in our woods.

Chapter Three

The wigwam

Philip and I left the path and fought our way through the young trees which seemed all tied together with honeysuckle. At last we paused to look round, and Philip sat down on some moss while I squatted beside him. "We'd better build our headquarters here," he announced. "It's a good base for further excavations."

Philip liked long words, and sometimes read the newspaper in search of them, though he did not always understand them.

"How?" I enquired.

"Like a wigwam," explained Philip. "Look, can you see that little mountain ash tree just there? That will be our centre prop. Now we'll collect branches, and lean them up against the middle, close together; then we'll tie them together with honeysuckle and just leave a little doorway to creep through – and we'll have a floor of dead bracken and moss, very soft and comfortable – it will almost be like building a nest. Then at the back we'll dig a hole and line it with sticks and stones. We'll bury our supplies there, and cover them with bracken so you won't be able to see anything; it will look just like a floor."

I was thrilled and set to work immediately. We worked hard all the morning, dragging dead boughs through the undergrowth and cutting long stakes with Philip's pen-knife. Before long we had the skeleton wigwam firmly fixed, with a little doorway just big enough to let a child through – though it was a tight squeeze even for Philip.

It took us some days to complete our wigwam; every morning I rushed through my jobs and we headed off for the woods. Every morning the pile of dust under the carpet grew bigger and bigger, but as Aunt Margaret had done the spring-cleaning my laziness was not noticed.

Oh, those mornings in the woods! We seldom kept together; we both wandered off on our own trail, happy with our own dreams, returning to the base with armfuls of bracken and honeysuckle binding – each of us finding our own treasures and adventures and sharing them on our return.

Perhaps our best find lay in the beech tree just above our wigwam. One day, when I was quietly weaving the wall, I heard a rush of great wings – a brown owl swooped close past me. I was up the trunk in an instant, like an excited squirrel, pulling myself from branch to branch and searching every hollow and crevice for the nest. My search was rewarded, for there, in the topmost fork of the tree, cradled in straw and fluffy brown feathers, lay one pure white egg, hot from the mother's breast.

I climbed down a little way, so as not to disturb the mother, and sat swinging my legs and looking about me. It was all so beautiful. I was so happy that it almost hurt – and then I saw Philip, looking very small, moving slowly through the trees, his arms full of bracken.

"Phil!" I called. "Come up here!"

He was up in a minute; together we gazed in deep delight at the pure, precious thing. Then we caught sight of the mother sitting in the next beech tree, snapping her yellow eyes angrily, and we thought we had better go down. Immediately, she spread her great brown wings and dropped onto her nest; we slid down and discussed baby owls, lying on our tummies in the wigwam.

Everything went well for a week. Aunt Margaret seemed happy enough to let us go our own way. If ever I noticed her looking tired and overworked, I told myself it was not my business. My holidays were my own; I was going to spend them how I pleased, and in any case I wasn't very good at housework. So it was rather annoying to me one morning when my aunt stopped me, just as I was tearing out of the house, and asked me where I was going.

"Out with Philip," I answered, wriggling as she held me. "I've done my jobs, honestly I have, Aunt Margaret. Please let me go; Phil's waiting for me."

"Well," replied my aunt quietly, "Philip must be content to go alone this morning. I need you, Ruth. I've got a big wash this morning, and you can help me. It's time you did a lot more than you do."

I kicked the ground and looked just about as miserable as it's possible for a child to look. "But I specially wanted to go out today," I whined.

"Well, you can just do what someone else wants for a change," she replied. "And if you can't do as you're told cheerfully, you can stay in this afternoon as well. You are getting more lazy and selfish every day; the sooner you change your ways, the better."

She marched off to the kitchen and I followed, scuffling my feet and scowling. I was furious. Why, the owl egg might hatch today, and I should miss it! It wasn't fair! I hated Aunt Margaret at that moment, and I made up my mind I wasn't going to help her. I'd be as naughty as I could and then she'd be sorry she'd ever asked me to stay.

My thoughts were interrupted by the back door being flung open and Philip's head appearing. He had been working for Uncle Peter in the garden, and he looked rather hot and untidy.

"Coming, Ruth?" he asked, eagerly.

"No, she's not coming," replied my aunt. "She's going to make herself useful for a change. You run and play by yourself this morning, Philip. Ruth can join you this afternoon, if she behaves herself."

We both had a miserable morning. I sighed and yawned and scuffled; I kicked the furniture and scowled at my aunt's back; but she was working hard at the wash-tub and pretended not to notice. She often pretended not to notice my tempers, and nothing annoyed me more. What was the good of being sulky when she would not even look at me? I grew crosser and crosser.

She noticed me all right in the end, however,

because she told me to carry out a basket of clean handkerchiefs and hang them on the line. I did not really mean to drop them, but I was so busy slamming the back door and rattling the clothes pegs that the basket slipped from my hands and all the handkerchiefs were scattered in the yard. It had rained in the night and the yard was very muddy.

My aunt was very angry indeed. I think she would have liked to slap me for I saw her clasp her hands very tightly together.

She told me the truth about myself in a furious voice. She said I could go now as I was more trouble than I was worth on a busy morning, but that for a whole week I was to stay in every morning and work in the house, and by the end of that time she hoped I would have learned how to be a little less clumsy. She spoke about my selfishness, and what a disappointment I should be to my mother. Then she took the basket of muddy handkerchiefs out of my hands and went into the house.

I stamped my foot, gulped back my tears, and marched out of the gate with my head in the air. I had lost my mornings for a week, but there was an hour left before dinner – I would go to meet Philip and walk home with him.

It was a very quiet morning, clouded and hazy and warm after rain; all the world smelt sweet and fresh. Flowers lifted their heads again, birds sang happily and I felt strangely out of place with my ugly, angry thoughts and my tear-stained face; so much so, that I even stopped to think about it, and looked about me. There were the trees, peacefully doing their work, each leaf unfolding perfectly. I couldn't have put it into words at the time, but that peace seemed to come inside me for a few minutes, and I stood thinking how perfect life could be if only I could be good.

I did not often want to be good, but I wanted it then – wanted with all my heart to be good, and happy, and useful. I even clasped my hands together and spoke aloud, because I wanted it so badly.

"I want to be good," I whispered. "I don't want to lose my temper and be selfish. Why can't I be good?"

But my words seemed to float away into the empty air, for I knew nothing of Jesus, the one who longed to help and change me. To me he was nothing more than a person who had lived long ago. I shrugged my shoulders and went on.

"I never shall be," I muttered. "I shall always be horrid and cross, and nobody will ever like me."

I met Philip, jumping about with joy. He did not seem to have missed me at all!

"I watched the egg hatch," he announced. "I went up and she flew off; when I looked, the shell was cracked and I could see the skin inside heaving up and down; I daren't stay in case it got cold and the owlet died. She's back now, brooding on it, but I shouldn't go up if I were you, because she might peck you."

There wasn't time to go up in any case, as it was time to go home to dinner. On the way I told Philip of my terrible morning. He was comforting and said how sorry he was, and I felt better, even though I knew perfectly well that I deserved no sympathy. Then, in his own thoughtful way, he stopped talking about the mornings and we spent the rest of our walk home planning the afternoons.

Chapter Four

Terry

It was only three days later that we had our first adventure and made a new friend. This is how it happened.

The wigwam was well and truly finished and as cosy a little house as anyone could wish for, with its secret hiding place where we hid our tea and other belongings when we were exploring. The owlet was growing – he now looked like a ball of soft grey cotton wool, with a hooked beak and round yellow eyes, and he didn't seem to mind us holding him in our hands.

The afternoon about which I am going to write was bright and windy; the wind was behind us, blowing strongly from the hills. We had been caught up in it and had run all the way. Being carried along like that had made us laugh, and we reached the wigwam quite breathless with running and laughter, ready to fling ourselves down on the mossy floor and get our breath back in the cool, dark shade of its walls. So it was quite a shock to me when Philip, who had dived half-way through the entrance, suddenly backed out, his eyes wide with astonishment, and whispered dramatically "The wigwam is occupied!"

"Who by?" I enquired crossly, backing a step or two.

"Well, I couldn't exactly see," replied Philip, "but I think its a boy."

"Well," I said loudly, "it's our wigwam, and he'd better come out, because we want to go in."

There was a dead silence.

"You'd better come out!" said Philip, very loudly and clearly.

Still no answer.

"Perhaps its a dead body?" I suggested.

"No, it isn't," answered Philip. "I saw it scratch itself."

There was a long, uncertain silence; Philip began to giggle.

"I think I'd better go in and look again," he said. "Perhaps he's deaf."

He went down on all fours and approached the entrance slowly and carefully. His front half disappeared into the doorway and another long silence followed.

"Hurry up!" I exclaimed impatiently, taking hold of his back legs in my excitement. "Who is he? And what is he doing?"

"We're just staring," said Philip with another giggle. "It's a boy, as I said. I say, boy, this is *our* wigwam, and we're coming in, so you'd better get out."

"Shan't!" said a voice from within.

"Then I shall pull you out," said Philip.

"Then I shall catch hold of the wall and pull it down with me," answered the voice coolly.

Another silence, while the rivals stared at each other and I danced up and down with excitement.

Philip broke the silence.

"I know," he said, "let's have a tournament, like in the history books!"

"A what?" enquired the voice; its owner didn't seem to know anything about history books.

"A tournament," repeated Philip. "It's like a fight between two people who are having a quarrel. Whoever wins the fight wins the quarrel. You come out and fight, and if I win you go away, but if you win you can share the hut. Because, after all, we *did* build it."

Our uninvited visitor seemed to like this idea, for I saw Philip wriggle out of the entrance backwards and roll over onto the ground, thus making room for him to come out. And angry as I was, the minute I saw his face in the gap I liked him, and wanted to get to know him.

"I hope Philip wins," I thought to myself. "But all the same, I hope he'll stay and play. I like him."

He was a little boy, about as big as me, but the same age as Philip. His clothes were ragged and rather too small for him, but his eyes were as bright as a blackbird's, and his thin face was very brown and covered with freckles. His thick hair fell down over his forehead and reminded me of an untidy thatch; in his arms he held an enormous bunch of kingcups and cowslips. He laid them carefully on the moss and told me to leave them alone while he "knocked out that toff."

The tournament began before anyone was ready for it, for the boy suddenly ran at Philip and punched him on the jaw. Philip, taken by surprise, didn't have time to hit back before he was punched again on the ear, and even then he stood and blinked several times before making up his mind what to do about it.

"Hit him, Phil!" I yelled, nearly joining in myself, and beating the nearest tree to relieve my feelings.

It was a good fight to watch, once Philip got started. Philip was as strong and determined as an ox, but the boy reminded me of a little ferret. He twisted and turned, and leaped and wriggled, his thin brown arms bulging with muscle, and his lips pressed tightly together. Back and back he came, while Philip stood his ground and measured out slow, steady blows. It was a very exciting tournament indeed, and I behaved like a whole crowd of spectators rolled into one.

The boy won; he pretended to spring at Philip's neck, and then suddenly changed tactics and dived between his feet, bringing him to the ground with an alarming crash. By the time Philip had realized what was happening, the boy was sitting on his chest, thumping him with all his might.

"Stop it!" said Philip, coolly, "You've won."

"Beat yer 'ollow!" said the boy, getting up. "But I don't want yer silly ol' hut. I could build a better one meself."

He was gathering up his flowers and making off when Philip ran over to him and held him.

"Don't go!" he said. "We'd quite like you to share the hut, and then perhaps one day we'll have another fight. I love fighting, don't you?"

"Not bad," said the boy.

"We're going to have tea now," urged Philip. "Come and have it with us. There's room for all three inside."

It was not nearly tea-time really, but we both felt we must do something to hang on to the boy – and at the word "tea" a remarkable change came over him. He stopped looking sullen and bored, and suddenly became interested. Without even troubling to say yes, he squatted down on the moss with an expectant smile on his face and held out his grubby hand. When he smiled, the light came into his eyes, and I thought he looked quite beautiful.

He must have been terribly hungry, for I have never seen anyone eat at such a speed either before or since! We opened our packet of sandwiches, and without so much as a please or thank you, he fell upon them and finished three while Philip and I were still eating our first, although our appetites were fairly healthy, too! When the last crumb had disappeared and he had licked the jam off the paper, we all settled down to get to know each other. We lay on our tummies, feeling sheltered and warm and peaceful.

"What's your name?" asked Philip.

"Terry," he replied, and went on chewing a piece of grass.

"How old are you?"

"Eleven in August."

"Where do you live?"

"At the cottage by the stream, down Tanglewoods way."

"Have you any brothers and sisters?"

"No – there's only me and Mum."

"Where's your father?"

"'Aven't got none."

"What are all those flowers for?"

"Me Mum sells 'em in the town – she's a flower-seller."

"Do you pick them all for her?"

"Yes, when I can skive off school."

Nobody spoke for a time, then I suddenly had an idea. I put my hand on his arm.

"Would you like to see an owl's nest?" I asked.

He pointed upwards to the tree. "That one?" he asked. "I've seen him once today; got a little tame one from that nest last year; it stopped with me for about two months."

I felt a little bit annoyed; it was our owl's nest, and he had no business to get there first. But Philip was before me. He leaned eagerly over towards the boy.

"Do you know lots of nests?" he asked. "Could you show us any more?"

He looked at us rather scornfully.

"I could show yer just about every nest in this 'ere wood," he replied.

Philip jumped to his feet. "Come on!" he cried. "Let's go and see! Show us them all, Terry!"

Terry got up slowly and looked us up and down, as though making up his mind whether we were the sort of children to be trusted with nests. Then he nodded.

"Right!" he answered briefly, and dived into the bushes.

A breathless hour followed, at the end of which I was quite exhausted and nearly torn to pieces, for Terry never stopped at an obstacle. We waded knee-deep in a pond to inspect a tree-warbler's woven home, and we climbed impossible trees in search of crow's nests. We inspected holes in trunks, and watched a starling fly in and out. We found out more about the wood in that hour than ever before. The sun was setting when we turned home.

"Good-bye," we said, and then we hesitated. Must this be the end? Would such a wonderful boy want to see us again?

"Coming again?" said Terry casually, and we heaved a great sigh of relief. From that moment Terry was our friend; and, better still, we knew that he looked on us as his friends.

Chapter Five

The lost lamb

We saw Terry nearly every day after that, and the time passed much too quickly. He led us all over the countryside and showed us his secret nests and lairs and burrows. We learned how to recognise and track the footprints of little animals and the different cries of birds and what they meant. He dragged us through swamps and marshes and brambles in search of the earliest flowers, and showed us where to pick orchids. It was as though he had opened up to us a whole new world of wonder, and we both loved and admired him because of everything he knew about life in the woods. Before, I had always disliked Philip's friends because I thought they took him away from me, but Terry seemed to think we were both equally his friends, and never looked down on me for being a girl, and younger than Philip and him.

So it was a disappointment to us all when Philip twisted his ankle while swinging from a tree, and, after hobbling home, had to lie on a sofa for three days.

I stayed at home at first to help amuse Philip; I believe my efforts were quite successful, but they nearly drove Aunt Margaret mad. I started by catching a duck and bringing him indoors, dressed up in a doll's hat, to visit Philip, and then letting him loose on the dining-room carpet.

After that, we decided to play soldiers and settled ourselves one at each end of the dining-room with an army of model soldiers and a dozen marbles each. We bombed each other quite happily for a time, then we suddenly thought that the four kittens in the woodshed would make excellent army horses. I trotted off, returning with an armful of soft, purring black and tabby fur, which I dropped on the carpet.

I chose a tabby and a black-and-white and Philip had two black ones for his army. We had a marvellous game, and the kittens loved it. They chased after the marbles in all directions, scattering soldiers right and left. Philip and I shrieked with laughter and scuttled round on our knees, collecting our ammunition and recapturing the "horses". Faster and faster ran the kittens, fiercer and fiercer grew the battle, when suddenly there was a crash and a splash – the tabby kitten had jumped onto a dangling tablecloth and pulled it, with a vase of flowers on top, all over himself. Philip and I laughed until the tears rolled down our faces. Of course, at that moment the door opened and Aunt

Margaret came in.

She was not amused. Four very excited little kittens were banished to the coal shed, and one very cross little girl was turned out of the house. Philip was given a book and put back on the sofa.

I decided to go to the woods and see if I could find Terry anywhere, so I squeezed through the gap in the hedge and strolled down the road.

I didn't go far into the wood, for the sun was pleasant on the outskirts and I wanted to pick flowers. I wandered round, dreaming of all sorts of things, until I had almost forgotten where I was, and it gave me quite a surprise to hear a man's voice quite close to me. I looked up quickly, but he was not calling me. He was standing with his back to me, peering into the bushes – he had not seen me at all. But I recognised him at once – it was Mr Tandy, the Cradley shepherd who had picked up the orphan lamb and carried it under his coat.

Being rather a "nosey" child, I wanted to know what he was doing, so I went and stood where he could see me. As soon as he saw me, he smiled broadly.

"Why!" he exclaimed, "you're the little girl who played with the lamb the other day – and here you are, turning up again just at the right moment. One of the little rascals has strayed, and I think he's got caught somewhere here in these bushes, but I just can't see where. Maybe you'll stop and help me find him."

I was delighted. Here was something nice to do, and a nice person to do it with, so I set to work happily. I liked this old man with his white hair and rosy face, and I felt he liked me; we were soon talking away as though we had known each other all our lives.

"Why did he stray?" I asked, as we parted the bushes and searched the ditches.

"Well," answered the old man, with a smile, "I reckon he's just like the rest of us; he likes his own way, and his own way has led him into trouble, poor little chap!"

"Well," I remarked, "I expect he's sorry for it now – all tied up in the bushes and wishing he'd stayed in his own field."

"Yes," agreed the old man, thoughtfully. "It takes a lot of thorns and briers to teach them lambs that their own way isn't the best one. He'll be crying his heart out for me now, maybe, if only I could find the place."

"Won't he be glad to see us!" I said. "Oh! I'm longing to find him! I expect he'll be very tired and hungry. Have you anything for him to eat?"

He put his hand into his pocket and drew out a bottle.

"You'll see!" he said. "The minute I pick him up in my arms he'll have his nose in my pocket. He knows I wouldn't forget him – the little rascal!"

He chuckled softly, and we moved farther into the wood.

"He's strayed a long way, hasn't he?" I remarked.

"True," answered the old man, "but I'll find him. I've found every lamb I've ever lost and brought them home. I always hear them crying out somewhere or other, although at times it's a very long search."

"What's the longest you've ever searched for?" I asked.

"Almost a whole night," he replied, "but that was in a storm, and I could hardly hear her crying for the wind and the thunder. She was caught fast in a bramble bush, and I found her at dawn by lantern light – almost dead with cold and hunger and crying."

"And what did you do?" I asked again.

"Do?" repeated the old man. "Why, I set her free and quietened her, and wrapped her in my coat, and carried her home. She was like a mad thing when we found her, but once she felt my arms around her she lay as quiet as a baby. She knew there was nothing to be afraid of then!"

I was about to ask another question, but he suddenly held up his hand and stood perfectly still, listening.

I had heard nothing, but his shepherd's ear had caught the sound at once – the faint cry of a tired lamb, calling for help.

"That'll be him," he said simply, "in those bushes." And he made straight for the sound.

It was a wonder to me, when we saw him, how the little creature had ever got in. The hedge was so tangled and the briers so thick; and it was a still greater wonder to me that the shepherd ever got him out. But we started off, parting the branches, and as he worked he spoke to the lamb as a mother might speak to a frightened little child.

I don't suppose the lamb understood the words, but he knew the voice at once, and knew in a flash that he had been searched for, and found and loved, and at the sound of it he stopped struggling and crying. He gave one joyful bleat and then lay still and waited.

It took a long time to reach him. I stood and watched as the old man patiently worked at the tangle, thorn by thorn, brier by brier. When he finally picked up the little rascal, his hands were dreadfully scratched and bleeding, but he didn't seem to notice. He just held that trembling lamb close and let it nuzzle its black nose trustfully into his pocket.

"Are you ready to come home?" he whispered, playfully lifting the little smudged face to his own.

"Baaa!" said the lamb, and put its nose back into the shepherd's pocket.

We walked home quietly together with the lamb lying in the crook of his arm. Mr Tandy seemed to be thinking deeply and his face looked very happy. When we reached the field, the sun was setting and the sky behind the bluebell slopes was the colour of pink shells. We laid the lamb among the others, and he gave a bleat of content and fell fast asleep.

"Well," I said slowly, "I suppose I'd better be getting home now. Thank you for letting me help, and I hope I'll see you again soon."

But he sat me down beside him on the wooden bench that ran round the outside of the sheep-fold. "Before you go, I'll read you a bit of a story about another sheep that strayed," he said. As he spoke, he took a small, worn Bible out of his pocket, and opened it at Luke, chapter fifteen, in the New Testament. Then he began to read, in his slow, kind, country voice.

I suppose I had heard the story before, but it had

never interested me. Tonight it was different, and I listened with all my heart.

"When he finds it, he is so happy that he puts it on his shoulders and carries it back home. Then he calls his friends and neighbours together and says to them, 'I am so happy I found my lost sheep. Let us celebrate!' In the same way, I tell you, there will be joy in heaven over one sinner who repents."

He closed his Bible and I looked up at him.

"Good-night, Ruth," he said.

"Good-night," I answered, "and thank you very much."

And I walked slowly home through the buttercups.

Chapter Six

A brilliant idea

I never told Philip about the shepherd – at least, not about the last bit – because I was afraid he would laugh and think it strange and I should not have liked that. In any case, I almost forgot about it next day, because I had one of my brain-waves, and when I had a brain-wave I could never think of anything else until I had carried it out.

It came about next day, when Philip was hobbling around the garden, not yet being able to walk to the woods. We had played all our usual games, and were lying under the apple trees wondering what to do next. As there wasn't anything much to do, we just lay and chatted, and Philip started talking about his book again.

"It's getting very fat, Ruth," he said, "and it's full of useful information about birds. All I'm waiting for now is the camera to take the pictures – and I shan't get it for years. Just think," he went on dreamily, "what a beautiful picture that baby owl would have made when he sat on our hands!

"Never mind," I said comfortingly, "we've got one shilling and ninepence more than when we last counted, so we're getting on!"

"But it's so slow," sighed Philip. "I shall soon be nearly grown up, and I expect I shall be sent to boarding school, and there won't be much chance to take pictures. I wish Auntie would let me be a delivery boy, and earn some money in my spare time."

I interrupted his thoughts by pouncing on him suddenly and slapping him violently on the back.

"Philip!" I shouted, "I've had a most marvellous idea!"

"What is it?" he asked doubtfully; he was a bit suspicious of my good ideas – they so often turned out badly, and ended up with punishments.

"It really is a good idea this time, Philip," I urged, "and Aunt Margaret could never find out. We'll pick flowers, like Terry's mother does, and sell them; we'll earn pounds and pounds. Do say yes, Phil! It would be such fun!"

Philip still wasn't at all sure about it.

"But Terry's mother wouldn't like it," he said, "Because if they bought our flowers they wouldn't buy hers as well, and then she wouldn't get so much money."

"Oh, but we won't go to the same places," I assured him. "She sells hers in the street in town; we'll go to people's back doors – and we'll dress up a bit to look like poor children."

Philip's eyes sparkled; he was beginning to agree with me, as I knew he would sooner or later.

"Let's go to the big houses half-way up the hill, where they have big iron gates and drives," he said. "We'll dress up in our oldest clothes and we'll make our faces a bit dirty and wear our muddiest shoes; you tie your plaits up in your red hanky, and we'll get pounds and pounds. Let's start soon!"

I always liked to carry out all my plans at once, and leapt to my feet immediately. Then I remembered Philip's ankle, and tried to slow myself down.

"You'll be able to walk tomorrow, won't you?" I pleaded.

"Although even if you couldn't, a little limp would be quite helpful. It would make people feel sorry for you. We could say 'Pity the poor lame beggar!' and hold out a hat, and you could put a big white hanky round your ankle and look as though it hurt you; only you wouldn't have to do it too much, because it would make me laugh."

Philip's ankle was much better next day, and we escaped early and made for the woods with a wicker shopping-basket. We were going to pick all the morning and sell all the afternoon. We had no idea of prices, which rather worried us, but we decided to guess and hope for the best.

"Where are you going?" I asked Philip, as we reached the stile.

"Down to the swamp in the hollow," he replied. "I'm going to pick lots of cowslips, and there are some late kingcups out. "We can get some wild cherry blossom, too," I added, "and I'm going to pick little bunches of wood sorrel and violets for tiny pots. We'll sell them very cheaply to the people who don't want big bunches. Oh, Phil! What fun it will be!"

I was dancing down the sloping path that led to the swamp, and nearly collided with a swinging bough of cherry blossom swaying low across the path. I stopped to pick some, and Philip caught me up. He did not help me, but stood quietly staring up at the pure clusters.

"Isn't it beautiful?" he remarked slowly. "It's like great snowdrifts up there. Isn't it a pity that it doesn't last? It will all have fallen in a few days, and the blossom will be all brown and ugly. Nothing beautiful really lasts, does it?"

"Oh, there'll be some bird cherries later on, I expect," I answered quickly. "Stop staring, Philip! It's silly to think about things like that; get on and pick some flowers – I'm doing all the work!"

Philip stooped down and started gathering large late violets, but his blue eyes were serious. I marched on rather crossly, for I didn't like Philip in these moods. But although I tried to forget them, his last words kept ringing in my ears; "Nothing beautiful really lasts, does it?"

It was quite true. All the nasty things like tempers and rows with Aunt Margaret went on and on, and you couldn't get rid of them; they might stop for a time, but you knew they would always come back; while beautiful things like holidays, and blossom, and sunsets, and birds singing, faded and died and left you feeling empty. Certainly other beautiful things came and took their places, but it didn't comfort you for the ones that had gone.

We picked hard all the morning, and filled the

shopping basket with our bunches of golden cowslips, vivid purple orchids and lacy white woodruff. The white blossom we left by itself, as we felt it looked perfect on its own. We hid all our flowers in the orchard, and went in to dinner, inwardly bubbling over with excitement, but outwardly quite calm.

Aunt Margaret looked rather hard at Philip, who was gobbling his dinner very fast. She wondered why we wanted to be off again so quickly.

"Philip," she said rather sharply, "I think you should rest that foot this afternoon. You've done enough walking on it this morning."

"Why, Auntie," he assured he in his most polite voice, "I've been standing nearly all the morning. I just went to the swamp and stayed there and picked a few flowers. I think, too," he added seriously, "that a lot of exercise makes it feel better. It stops it getting stiff. In fact, I had planned to walk on it as much as possible this afternoon."

And Philip, as usual, had his way, as he always did with Aunt Margaret.

"Very well," she agreed, "but don't overdo it – and keep out of that swamp; your sister's shoes are a perfect disgrace."

Philip looked at my shoes and sighed. He, of course, had remembered to change his before Aunt Margaret noticed them. I, of course, had not. How much easier life would be, I thought, if I had been born like Philip!

Aunt Margaret went into the kitchen to wash up after dinner. She did not ask me to help her, and I certainly did not offer. I was always full of excuses and arguments when asked to help, and my aunt was rather tired today, so she left me alone.

Once the door was firmly closed, I fled upstairs. I untwisted my plaits, and my hair fell dark and loose to my waist. Then I tied up my head in my Indian handkerchief that Mum had sent me and put on a dirty apron. My muddy shoes needed no touching up. I looked a perfect little vagabond. Philip wore his bird's nesting coat and Wellington boots and looked just the right companion for me.

"Don't let Aunt Margaret see us," he whispered as we slipped out of the door. "She'd have fifty fits! We'd better go through the gap."

We climbed the hill that led to the big houses rather slowly, for the day was hot and the basket was heavy; also, Philip's ankle hurt quite a bit, although he would not admit it. What really worried us was the fact that the flowers were drooping so much. Of course, we should have put them in water straight away.

Although we hadn't been able to wait to sell the flowers, when we actually reached the first pair of iron double gates we seemed in no hurry to go in.

"What are you going to say?" asked Philip, rather nervously.

"Me?" I replied. "I'm not going to say anything. You've got to say it. You're much better at all that sort of thing than me."

"Oh, well," replied Philip peaceably, "perhaps we shan't have to say anything. Perhaps the person who lives here will come to the door and say 'What beautiful bunches of flowers! I'll buy two,' – and then we shall just smile and hand them over, and she'll give us some money and we'll go away."

This thought cheered us up a lot, and we walked

rather quicker until the path divided; the left-hand path ran round the front between beautiful lawns, flower beds and cedar trees; the right-hand one ran round to the back.

"Do we go front or back?" I asked.

"Back, I think," said Philip. "After all, we mustn't forget we're flower-sellers."

Our timid knock at the back door sounded dreadfully loud – so loud that we both jumped. The door was flung open by a very grand housemaid with dyed, curly hair, who smelt of perfume.

"Well?" she asked, sharply.

I turned away from Philip with shaking shoulders as I couldn't stop laughing but not before I had seen that he was feeling as bad as I was. He pulled out his handkerchief and pretended to sneeze into it.

"Well?" she asked again. This time she sounded really angry, so Philip controlled himself and answered in a very shaky voice.

"Would you like to buy some flowers?" he squeaked.

"Good gracious, no!" replied the girl. "What in the world would we be buying flowers for here? Anyway, those what you've got in the basket are all dead."

"Oh, they'll be all right in water..." I began, but she had already slammed the door in our faces, and we were left giggling weakly on the steps.

The next house certainly looked less grand; the garden was smaller, and we could see the front door from the road. We stopped a minute to read a notice on the gate. It said "NO HAWKERS, NO CIRCULARS" in large capital letters.

"What does that mean?" I asked.

"I don't know," answered Philip. "It sounds like a man that sells hawks. Anyhow, it couldn't mean us, so come on!"

We walked on up the path, holding the basket between us. "Whatever happens, we mustn't laugh this time," said Philip.

We rang the bell much louder than we should have done. An old lady with an eye-glass and a very straight back opened the door and stood looking down at us as though she didn't like us much.

We were so determined to get it right this time that we both started talking at once, very fast and loud.

All the time we were talking the old lady stood staring at us in astonishment. She took no notice of the withered bunch of cowslips that I was trying hard to push into her hand, and asked in a cold voice: "Little boy and girl, did you not read the notice on the gate?"

"Yes," admitted Philip, rather puzzled, "but I'm not a hawker."

"And I'm sure I'm not a circular," I added, rather cheekily.

"Little girl and boy," went on the old lady in a very posh voice, "if you're too young to understand the English language, you are certainly too young to be doing this sort of thing. Go home to your mother!"

And for the second time that day we found ourselves standing on the steps with the door shut in our faces.

Philip was fed up and disappointed, and suggested going home; but I wasn't ready to give up yet.

It was at this point that a man came round the corner, and nearly bumped into us.

Philip was watching a skylark.

"Are you interested in birds?" asked the man suddenly.

"I'm extremely interested in them," replied Philip, "Are you?"

"Very," answered the man. "I have all sorts of birds nesting in this garden. I'll show you some if you like."

Philip walked away with the man, already chatting seriously about birds, and I followed with the flowers.

We had a very happy half hour, for he showed us four or five rare nests, and Philip was in his seventh heaven. Then, when we had been all round the garden, he took us on to the verandah and gave us each a drink of lemonade. As we drank it, he suddenly remarked, "By the way, why did you come?"

Philip had quite completely forgotten the real reason for our visit, and looked quite startled for a moment. So I answered for him, holding out the basket.

"We came to sell flowers," I explained, "Would you like to buy some?"

He chose three bunches of dying cowslips.

"Is this how you earn your living?" he asked.

"Oh no," I replied, "not really; we wanted to earn some money for something very particular, so we thought we'd sell some flowers – but nobody seems to want them."

"Nonsense!" said the man. "Cowslips are my favourite flowers, I'd pay a lot for a scent like that" – and he pressed two shillings into my hand.

Philip went rather pink. Then laying his hand on the man's sleeve, he said earnestly, "We should like to give them to you. You have given us such a love-ly afternoon, and... and... we are very grateful to you."

The last words came out with a rush, as though he was reading a speech. The man's eyes twinkled, but he still spoke seriously.

"Not at all," he replied. "It's been a pleasure to meet you, and I should like your little sister to keep the money. You have an excellent knowledge of birds for someone so young, and I should like you to come again."

I put the two shillings in my pocket in a great hurry. I was afraid the man would do as Philip had said, but he didn't. He walked to the gate with us, and we all shook hands and said thank you. Then he turned back up the drive and we stood once again in the road.

"Let's go home," said Philip.

"All right," I agreed. "Two shillings isn't bad for a first day, and we will try again tomorrow."

But Philip did not answer; he was walking down the road in a happy dream. He had been in Paradise.

Chapter Seven

An unfortunate tea-party

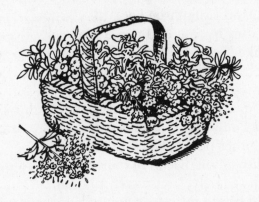

We went out flower-selling nearly every afternoon after that, for a week, and earned nearly fifteen shillings. We never again met anyone quite so nice as the bird man, but quite a lot of people seemed pleased with our flowers and bought bunches. We told Terry what we were doing and he did not mind at all; in fact, he helped us quite a lot because he knew just what colours to put together, and how to arrange them. So that Aunt Margaret should not see the flowers, we kept the bucket by a gap in the hedge, and Terry would sometimes arrive there late in the evenings and add a few of his flowers to ours. We had shown him our private gap as a sign of friendship, and he used to creep in and out and leave notes for us. His spelling was bad, but that did not worry us at all.

Most mornings we found a scrap of paper which said, "Cum to △ bring ooooo." This meant that Terry would be waiting for us at the wigwam and would need some food.

It was towards the end of the week, when we were sitting at dinner, that my aunt remarked:

"I'm going out to tea this afternoon, Philip and Ruth, and I shan't be back till about six. You may take your tea out and not come back till supper, if you like."

We both did like, very much, and we kicked each other joyfully under the table.

"Who are you going out to tea with, Auntie?" asked Philip, who always took a polite interest in what other people were doing.

"With an old friend of mine who has come to live here just lately," answered my aunt. "Later on, I should like to introduce you to her; she is very fond of children and has often asked about you. She knew your mother, too."

"Will she ask us out to tea too?" I asked with interest. I liked going out to tea because we always had such nice things to eat.

"If she did, you would have to behave yourself rather better than you usually do," replied my aunt, and I frowned and wriggled with annoyance. Why should she always spoil even nice, good things like going out to tea with silly remarks like that? Of course I always behaved nicely when asked out to tea! I was far too shy not to, and in any case it was rather fun having grown-ups say how well-mannered we were; quite a change, too, as far as I was concerned.

When dinner was over, my aunt took me off to

the kitchen to help dry up the dishes, which I did at lightning speed, and ran off the moment I'd finished. Aunt Margaret called after me to come back and put the cloth away tidily, but I pretended not to hear and scuttled through the front door.

Philip was waiting near the gap, looking rather worried, with the basket in his hand.

"Come along, " he said, "we must get well away before Auntie starts. We might meet her – and we forgot to ask which way she was going."

"Oh, I think she's going down the town way," I answered carelessly. "I heard her say something to Uncle Peter about it – someone she was going to see down Beech Road."

"But perhaps it was somebody else," said Philip.

"No, no," I replied, "it was sure to be the same one. She doesn't go and see many people; she's too busy."

Philip chewed a piece of grass thoughtfully.

"She's always working, isn't she?" he remarked at last. "Sometimes I think we should help her a bit more than we do. After all, it's quite kind of her to have us to live with her; we're not her children."

"Oh, I don't know," I answered quickly, for this sort of talk was not at all to my liking. "I help with the drying and dusting sometimes, and you do the wood for Uncle Peter, and we both pick fruit in summer, and shell peas and things. After all, we're not grown-ups, and children shouldn't have to work in the holidays. We do quite enough work in the term."

But I could see by the look on Philip's face that he was not quite satisfied, so I changed the subject as soon as possible.

We went down a country road today, to a collection of rather pretty cottages. At the first four houses everyone bought something, and we earned over two shillings.

It was a peaceful sort of day on which no one would expect anything to happen; and so we were taken completely by surprise, never dreaming that the afternoon would turn out as it did.

We wandered up a lane to have tea, and sat on a gate looking over a bright buttercup field, where sleepy brown cows chewed their cud and switched their tails lazily. We munched our bread and jam as peacefully as the cows and almost as silently, for Philip was not really a talkative boy.

It was still only four o'clock, so we decided to go back to the road and try some more cottages. We were going to do our best today, and then go back to Terry and the woods tomorrow, for we were getting a little tired of flower-selling. Still, it was encouraging to be finishing up so well, and on reaching the road we approached the next cottage hopefully enough.

It was a very nice one, long, low and built of grey stone. We walked up the path and along to the front door; on our way we passed under a window, and heard the clink of china and the sound of ladies' voices. It sounded as if some sort of a tea-party was going on, and ladies at tea-parties are usually in rather a good mood, as Philip wisely remarked.

We rang the bell, and the lounge door opened immediately. A young lady came out and stood looking at us for a moment before asking us what we wanted. When we held out the basket and asked her to buy some flowers, she started to smile.

"Wait a minute, " she said, instead of answering our question, "I must ask my mother, and then you must come in and show us what you've picked."

She disappeared back into the lounge, and we heard her merry laugh as she told her mother about us.

"Such a cute little couple, pretending to be flower-sellers," we heard her say. "The boy has a face like an angel, and the girl looks like a little wild thing. You must see them for yourselves – I'll bring them in."

She came back, smiling, and held out her hand.

"Come in a moment," she said, "and show my mother and aunt your basket. I'm sure they would like to buy some cowslips. You shall have a biscuit each, too. We're just having tea."

We trotted in after her, suspecting nothing, and then we both stopped still suddenly in the doorway, struck with horror.

There were four chairs placed round a little table in the window so that the ladies were sitting with their backs to us. In the first chair sat a tall, elderly lady who was evidently the mother, for she was pouring out the tea; next to her sat the aunt, and next to her was the empty seat which was about to be occupied by the young lady.

Next to that was a high-backed armchair, with large sides, and from it came the unmistakable voice of Aunt Margaret.

"The little girl is very rough," said the voice. "I shall be only too glad when her mother comes and takes her off my hands."

"Run!" I whispered to Philip. "Oh, Phil, run quick!"

But Philip in his usual slow fashion had not yet realised what had happened; he stood there blinking as though he were in some puzzling dream. I tried to think of another way to escape.

There was one small hope; if we walked in and stood behind my aunt's chair, it was quite impossible for her to see us for the chair was very big; but if we were asked to speak, she would certainly know it was us. However, it was our only chance. As the young lady was beckoning us to come forward, wondering why we were hesitating, I took Philip's hand and led him to the only safe spot in the room.

The older lady smiled and tried to make us feel at home. She held out her hand for a bunch of cowslips; I took two steps forward, leaned right over, pushed them at her, and scuttled back to my hiding-place like a frightened rabbit to its burrow. The girl looked rather surprised, for we had not seemed shy on the doorstep; yet here we were behaving in the most peculiar fashion, and Philip was standing like a stuffed dummy, with his mouth open.

"What beautiful big flowers!" said Mrs Sheridan, examining them, "we shall have to go exploring and find some, too; whereabouts did you pick these, children?"

There was dead silence; neither of us dared speak. I heard a rustle in the armchair as though my aunt was about to turn round and examine these strange dumb children behind her – and if her head suddenly appeared over the top I knew I would scream. So I replied, in a hoarse whisper, "In the hollow, by the stream."

"By the stream," repeated Mrs Sheridan. "Yes, I might have known these had grown near water; I shall certainly buy a bunch. Fetch my purse, Isobel, and give these two children a biscuit each before they go."

The girl held out the plate, but to reach it we should have to walk out in the open. We shook our heads frantically, but she just thought we were being polite.

"Come along," she said, laughing, "they're very nice biscuits."

Hopelessly I took two steps forward, and leaned over as far as I could to grab two biscuits; but as I did so I saw my aunt's hat move, and I leapt backwards. I bumped into a small cake stand and sent it flying.

My aunt's head appeared round the side of the chair and she saw me.

I can only dimly remember what happened next. I heard my aunt shout, "Philip and Ruth, what is the meaning of this?" and Mrs Sheridan say, "Pick them up, Isobel – they are butter-side down all over the carpet – don't let them get trodden in!"

I saw Philip move back and trip over Isobel, who was picking up buttered buns, and I noticed that her face looked as though she was trying not to laugh. I remember everybody apologising for everybody, and my aunt saying she could not understand it, a great many times, and Mrs Sheridan saying it was nothing to worry about, and we were to forget all about it.

The next thing that comes back clearly to me, was my aunt turning to us when all the fuss had died down, and telling us she was taking us home to punish us most severely; but before we went we were to come forward and tell Mrs Sheridan how sorry we were for behaving so badly.

Philip had recovered by now, and he stepped forward immediately and looked up into Mrs Sheridan's face. He was truly sorry for having spoilt such a nice tea-party, especially when Aunt Margaret went to so few, and he said so, so earnestly and politely that everyone was charmed; even my aunt looked pleased and if only she could have stopped there, all would have ended peacefully; but now she turned to me and asked me coldly what I had to say for myself.

I don't quite understand to this day why I was so angry, but while Philip was talking, I had decided that my aunt was an idiot; there was no need to have recognized and owned us – we should never have shown we belonged to her, and then no one would have known. Therefore, I argued, she had brought all this trouble on herself, and here we were being told we were naughty, in front of everyone – and we weren't naughty – why shouldn't we sell flowers? Anyone would think we were stealing!

All this was flashing through my angry little heart when my aunt spoke to me. I stuck my hands in my pockets and stamped my muddy boot.

"I'm not a bit sorry," I said. "We're not doing anything wrong, and no one called us naughty till we met you. We've earned the money and it belongs to us, and we shall go on doing it if we want. You always spoil everything, Aunt Margaret."

My aunt went quite white; never in my worst moments at home had I spoken to her like this, and here I was disgracing us all in somebody else's front room. I suddenly felt terrified and miserable, and ran out into the garden, leaving them all standing looking at each other.

I wanted to dash on, but realised that they might think I was running away, and I was far too proud to run away. So I walked off towards home with my hands in my pockets, and my head held very high in the air. I knew my aunt and Philip were coming down the hill behind me, so I pretended to whistle, but I was too miserable to keep it up for long. When I reached home I went and stared out of the kitchen window and tried to whistle again; I wanted to look as though nothing had happened, and as though I didn't care if it had. Above all, I wasn't going to be sorry.

My aunt came in slowly, as though she was very, very tired. She came and stood beside me, looking out of the window.

"Ruth," she said slowly, "I'm not going to punish you, because it doesn't seem to do much good, but I've been thinking it out on the way home. I don't seem able to manage you, or bring you up as I should. You have ten days' more holiday, and then, if they can take you, I am going to send you to boarding school. Your mother suggested it at Christmas, but I wanted to keep you then. Of course, it will be a big extra expense, but anything is better than have you grow up selfish and stubborn and bad-mannered as you are now."

She turned away without looking at me, and I went on staring out of the window. I felt as though the whole world was falling down round me, and I wanted to run to Philip and bury my face in his sweater and cry, as I used to when I was a tiny girl. But Philip had been sent straight upstairs to bed, and I was alone.

"I shan't go," I said, in what was meant to sound a strong voice, but which only sounded small and shaky.

"You won't be asked," replied my aunt, quietly.

There was a long silence, and I stood perfectly still, thinking furiously. Then I spoke again in the same small, trembling voice that tried so hard to be proud.

"Very well," I announced, "I shall run away, and I shan't come back." And with that I ran straight out of the door and into the road.

My aunt took no notice. It was very early, and I often rushed off like this in a temper. No doubt I would come back before dark. She sighed heavily and went slowly up to her room.

Chapter Eight

Running away

I did not stop for a minute when I got out into the road; I just went on running. It did not matter to me where I went so long as I got away, and in my angry heart I decided that I would never, never go back again. I would get some kind lady to adopt me, or ask someone to let me be their little servant, and then perhaps Aunt Margaret would be sorry. I knew Uncle Peter would miss me when he came home every night, and of course Philip would be dreadfully sad. At the thought of Philip I started to cry, and I went on running and running with the tears streaming down my cheeks.

"You're going away to boarding school." I kept whispering the horrid words to myself, and trying to take it all in. I saw myself going away in disgrace, alone in a train to a building which I

imagined would be rather like a prison. I imagined
Terry and Philip sitting in the wigwam together,
with the birds singing and the foxgloves sprouting
up above the bracken and I should not be there.
Then other pictures seemed to dance before my
eyes; Philip kneeling alone at the bedroom window
with the sun rising over the hills – and my little bed
empty; Philip lying on his tummy in the hayfields,
writing his book – and I should not be there to
draw the pictures.

It was quiet all around me as I trotted along. I
had met no one, and except for the cries of birds
going to bed and my own sobbing, the world had
seemed quite silent. But now I suddenly realised I
could hear children's voices and dogs barking.

I had reached the entrance to a village where I
had been once or twice before. It was a very little
village; only a few cottages, a school, a village shop
and a church.

I stood for a little while wondering what to do. I
was hot and very tired, and my head was beginning
to ache. I wanted to sit somewhere cool and quiet,
where I could rest, and think where to go next. I
looked all round me and then realised that I was
standing by a little brown wooden gate that led
into a church yard, and the church door was open.
No one was likely to go into church as late as this,
and even if they did I could crouch down in a pew,
and they would not see me; so I went up the path
between the rows of quiet gravestones, reading the
names as I went past.

One stone interested me specially, and I stopped
to read it again. It was a little white cross, marking
a garden of forget-me-nots. On it was written,

"JANE COLLINS, AGED 9 YEARS, WENT TO BE WITH THE LORD, APRIL 5TH, 1900."

I read it through several times, and then shivered at the thought of poor little Jane Collins who had died so young, and in April, too, so she would have left behind the spring sunshine, lambs and flowers. Death had always seemed a long way ahead, something to be thought about by old people and clergymen, but Jane Collins was only nine years old when she "went to be with the Lord." What if I, aged nine, had suddenly to go and "be with the Lord"? What would he say to me about all my tempers, and the lies I told, and the times I'd run away instead of helping, and the dust under the carpet. It would be far, far worse than going to boarding school. For the first time in my life I began to feel really frightened about being so naughty.

I walked on into the church porch, and peeped inside. It was quite empty, so I slipped through the door and began wandering round looking at all the things on the walls. One thing pleased me most of all – and that was the evening light streaming through the stained-glass windows and falling in coloured patterns on the stone floor.

As I stood watching, it suddenly came over me how dreadfully tired I was. The church was so quiet and cool and friendly, with its sunset light and its daffodils, that I thought I would lie down and rest a little before deciding what to do next. I collected some footstools, made a little mattress, wrapped myself up in an old black gown that hung near the door, and cuddled down inside one of the pews where I could watch the beautiful patterns and think things out.

But I had not realised how sleepy I was. I had been out in the open air all day. I had been very frightened and very angry and very miserable, and I had run nearly three miles on a warm spring evening. All these things were enough to make any little girl dog-tired; in fact, I was so tired that I could hardly remember laying my head down on the footstool before all my cares melted away from me, and I knew I couldn't keep awake any longer.

But just as I was dropping off, I thought I saw Jane Collins standing in the sunset light of the west window, pointing upwards along the golden rays; she was a little girl just like me, with dark plaits and a pinafore and blue socks, and the moment I saw her face I knew I had made a mistake in pitying her, for never before, either in dreams or real life had I seen a child look so radiantly happy. Her arms were full of Easter flowers, and somehow I knew perfectly well that they would never fade or die. Then the light grew dim and blurred and I fell into a deep, deep sleep.

When I woke up I was lying in the dark, and for a long time I could not imagine where I was. I was very stiff, and cold, and sore, for the footstools had come apart and I was lying partly on the stone floor. I sat up and changed my position. Directly I lifted my face I found that a wonderful thing had happened; the day was beginning to dawn, and a grey light was coming through the eastern window on the other side of the church; the darkness had scattered, and with it all my terrors and nightmares. I gave a great sigh of relief and sat quite still facing the morning light.

As I sat there waiting and listening, the dreadful

silence was broken by the clear call of one bird, and I realised with a thrill of joy that the world was waking up again after the terrible night. Then another bird woke and answered, then another, until it seemed as if every bird in Herefordshire must be singing; and as I sat listening, the grey light gave place to gold. The sun was rising, and morning had come again.

The relief was so great that I did not want to move. I forgot that I was cold and hungry and only remembered that the night was over, and that I was no longer alone, because the birds had woken up. Soon I would slip out of the church and run home to Philip, but for the moment I was content to sit and listen.

But I did not sit and listen for long, for somehow my head fell over onto the footstools and I dropped fast asleep again. When I woke the next time it was very suddenly, for the church was flooded with light, and there were heavy footsteps coming up the aisle.

I sat quite still and waited as the footsteps came nearer, and then my curiosity got the better of me; I crawled to the edge of the pew and peeked over. It was the clergyman; he was walking slowly up the church, looking up at the eastern windows. He need not have seen me at all, for his head was turned away and I was quite small enough to creep under the seat. I was just about to do this, for I did not want to be seen. Children were not allowed to sleep in churches, I was sure, and there was a police station just down the road. But I had been lying all night in a cold church with my legs on a stone floor, and I had caught a cold, so I was only half out of sight when a dreadful thing happened.

I sneezed!

I tried to stop, but it was no use; out it came with a loud explosion, and the clergyman jumped. Then he came and looked over the side of the pew. He said nothing, but came inside and sat down; then he leaned over and spoke very gently.

"Come out," he said. "There's no need to hide under the seat. I don't mind children in my church."

I uncurled slowly, sat down on the seat beside him, and looked up into his face. He was not very young and not very old, and his eyes were blue and kind. He reminded me of the old shepherd some-how – the sort of man I was not afraid of talking to.

"I couldn't help being here," I explained. "I came in last night when the door was open, and I went to sleep by mistake. I put on your gown because I was cold, but I didn't mean to stay all night. Only when I woke up the first time it was too dark to move, and when I woke up again it was morning."

He looked rather startled. "Do you mean that you have been here all night?" he asked. "Whatever is your mother thinking? We must let her know where you are at once."

I sat silent for a moment, twisting my hands together. I had a sudden feeling that I wanted to tell someone all about it, and I thought this man would do.

"It's not my mother," I whispered, "it's my aunt; I wouldn't have done it with my mother. I've been very, very naughty, and she's going to send me away to boarding school because she can't manage me, and I didn't want to go, so I ran away, and here I am."

I looked up to see if he was very shocked, but he didn't seem to be. He just looked very interested and rather sorry for me.

"I'm glad you told me that," he said, "and I should like you to tell me a great deal more about it. But first of all we must tell your aunt where you are; perhaps, when she knows you're safe, she will let you stay a little while, and we can talk. Are you on the 'phone?"

We were, and I knew the number.

"Good," said my friend, "we'll go straight back to the vicarage, ring up your aunt, and tell her all about it."

I put my small hand into his large one, and we walked out of the church together. The world was full of bird-song and light and colour, but I knew it must be very early morning because the flower petals were still closed.

"Why did you come to church so early?" I asked suddenly.

"I came to say my prayers," answered the clergyman. "I often come out early, because everything looks so beautiful. Don't you think that these buttercups are enough to make anyone feel good and happy?"

I looked at the buttercups, but I did not feel happy, and I was quite certain I should never be good.

Chapter Nine

I make a new friend

"We went into the vicarage and he took me straight to his study. It was a big sunny room, full of books, and while I sat and rested in a big armchair he went away to telephone. He was gone a long time, and having nothing else to do I wandered round the room looking at the pictures. They were mostly photographs and not very interesting, but there was one which I liked so much that I moved my chair over in front of it so that I could gaze at it.

It was the picture of a sheep lost on a rocky mountainside. Overhead hovers a fierce bird, waiting for it to die, and the sheep looks up and cries to be rescued. Someone has heard its cry, for the shepherd with his crook is leaning over the edge; in another moment he will pick it up and carry it safe home in his arms.

I was looking at the picture so closely that I never noticed that the clergyman had come back. Now he stood in front of me with a tray which he laid down beside me.

"I've telephoned your aunt," he said. "She's been very worried about you and the police and your uncle have been out looking for you all night. However, now she knows you're safe, she doesn't mind you staying to breakfast with me. Then you must go home and tell her how sorry you are."

I fell upon the tray of food with a tremendous appetite, for I had had nothing to eat since the day before. It was such a nice breakfast, too, with a boiled egg and strawberry jam and a teapot all to myself. I munched away happily. The vicar sat down on the sofa while I ate my breakfast, and we talked. I told him all about Philip and Terry, and the bird book, and the wigwam, and the camera, and the flower-selling. He asked a great many questions and seemed really interested in it all.

But when I had finished my last mouthful of bread and jam, I realised that now I should probably be sent straight home, and I didn't want to go just yet for I thought my new friend was one of the nicest men I had ever met, except perhaps Mr Tandy, the old shepherd. So I laid down my tray and went over and sat down beside him on the sofa; once again I found myself staring at the picture on the wall.

"Isn't that a nice picture?" I remarked. "It reminds me of the shepherd at home. One of his lambs escaped, like the one in the picture, and he went back to look for it. I went, too; we looked for ever so long, and then we found it all tangled up in a thorn bush, and it took Mr Tandy ages to get it out; his hands got all scratched to bits in the thorns."

My friend was looking at the picture, too; he did not answer for a minute.

"Ruth," he said suddenly, "how did the lamb get into such a place? Why did he ever get lost?"

"Well," I replied, "I suppose he ran away; they often do."

"Yes," went on the clergyman – and he was speaking very seriously now. "But why did he run away? He had a kind shepherd and a very nice green field. Why didn't he stay there?"

"Well," I answered thoughtfully, "I expect he thought it looked nicer outside, and went to see. Then I expect he got lost, and when he wanted to go back he just couldn't find the way."

"You're quite right," said my new friend. "Just look at the lamb in the picture. I expect he had been trying to find his way back all night; but he was lost and the farther he went, the steeper the rocks became and the more hopeless he felt. So I think he stopped trying at last, and just stood quite still at the edge of the precipice; and what did he do then, Ruth?"

I looked up at him; I was beginning to understand that he was not talking about a real sheep any longer. "I don't know," I whispered, rather shyly.

"Well, then, I'll tell you," went on my friend. "I think he looked round and saw a precipice underneath him and big rocks above him, and he said to himself, "it's no good, I can't possibly get back by myself. There's only one person who can take me home – and that's the shepherd. So he opened his mouth and gave a little cry. The shepherd had been waiting all night for that little cry; as soon as he heard it he leant over and picked up the lamb, and carried it safe back to his own field. And I don't know who is the happier, the lamb or the shepherd."

My eyes were fixed on him; I knew now that he was talking about me.

"I ran away, too, and got lost last night, didn't I?" I whispered again.

"You did," answered the clergyman, "and you'll never find your way back on your own, Ruth. There's only one person who can take you back into God's way and keep you there, and that is the Lord Jesus Christ, who called himself the Good Shepherd.

"Every time you are naughty, you are getting a little bit farther away from God's way, and a little bit more lost than you were before. What you have to do is to stop trying to make yourself good. You have to tell the Shepherd that you are quite lost, and ask him to find you."

"Will he really do it?" I asked.

"Ruth," said the clergyman suddenly, "how old are you?"

"Nine," I answered, wondering what that had to do with it.

"Well then, he's been loving you and looking for you for nine whole years; don't you think he'll be glad to hear you call to him, when he's been waiting for such a long time?"

I sat very still, thinking hard.

"Is it really all I've got to do to be good?" I asked at last. "I thought it was very difficult to be good."

"It's all you must do at first," he answered, "that's the wonderful part. You see, the Good

Shepherd has done it all for you. He took away sin when he died on the cross, so that you can be forgiven without any punishment. You told me that your friend's hands got dreadfully torn and scratched as he rescued that lamb – but he lifted it out of the thorns without hurting it at all. And in just the same way Jesus, the Good Shepherd, was wounded and hurt when he came to look for you. He has done everything, and all you have to do is say thank you, and believe that his wounded hands can lift you up and carry you back to God's fold the moment you ask him."

"And what happens then?" I asked. "Will I always be good after that?"

"You won't always be good all at once," he replied, "but you will always belong to the Good Shepherd, Jesus, and he will begin to teach you how to be good. He will often speak to you in your heart, and you must learn to listen to his voice. When he speaks you must always try to obey. And you must learn to talk to him about everything, too. We call it praying, but really it means sharing everything with Jesus."

Once more we sat still for a long time. At last the clergyman spoke.

"I have to go to my church now," he said gently, "and you must go home, or your aunt will think you've run away to somewhere else. But before you go I'm going to give you a copy of that picture for your very own. Take it with you and look at it often, and each time you look at it remember that you are that lost lamb and that the Good Shepherd is waiting to find you as soon as you ask him. One other thing – have you a Bible of your own?"

I said I had a Bible in my drawer at home.

"Then when you get home find the Gospel of St Luke and read a bit every night. It will tell you all the story of the Shepherd and how he came to earth to look for lost sheep. And when you've finished it, read the other Gospels: Matthew, Mark and John."

He opened a drawer and took out a postcard-sized copy of the picture on the wall. I took it with shining eyes, and whispered, "Thank you."

I followed him out, holding my new treasure tightly. He came to the gate and stood watching me as I set out along the road. When I had gone a little way, I turned round and ran back. "Shall I come back and tell you when it's happened?" I asked.

He nodded. "I was hoping you would," he admitted. "I shall always be glad to see you, so come whenever you like."

So I left him and turned the corner. The road ahead of me led back home. At the thought of home my heart beat rather fast. What would my aunt and uncle say to me, and what would I say to them?

But I did not worry very much, for I had more important things to think about. In my hand was the picture, and in my heart I had decided what I was going to do. I would find some quiet place far away from everyone, and before I went back home I would ask the Good Shepherd to find me and make me one of his lambs.

I was very fussy about the spot; I didn't want to be seen from the road and I wanted to be quite alone. So I walked on until I came to the woods and slipped in and out among the trees till I reached a little clearing right away from any path. Here I knelt down and felt as though I was in some secret chapel, far away from the world. I looked again at my picture, but at first I dared not pray. I felt as if my whole life was going to depend on the next few moments. What if I spoke and nothing happened? What if the Good Shepherd had gone away and was not listening any more?

Then I spoke aloud to the Good Shepherd. I told him about my naughtiness, and how I couldn't be good by myself. I told him I was sorry because I'd kept him waiting so long, and then I asked him to forgive me and find me and pick me up in his arms, and never let me run away from him again.

Then I waited, perfectly still, for my answer, almost expecting to feel the gentle arms thrown around me. And what happened? I heard nothing, I felt nothing, but I knew deep inside that my prayer was heard. I knew that at that moment I had been searched for, and loved and found.

I was so happy that I stayed where I was for a long time, as though if I moved I would break some spell. I was not only happy, I was thankful, too. I remembered how long he had waited, and I thought of Mr Tandy's poor, bleeding hands, and remembered how Jesus' hands had been wounded when he died on the cross for me.

Then I remembered that I was supposed to be going home; my aunt was waiting for me. So I left my special little place and went back to the road.

But I walked very slowly. Would they be very angry with me? Worst of all, would I be naughty and rude again? My rudeness seemed to come out whether I wanted it to or not, and if I was naughty now everything would be spoilt.

Then I remembered something else; the Good

Shepherd had picked me up in his arms, and I could tell him everything if he was really as close to me as all that. So I told him all about it as I trotted home, and somehow all my happiness came back to me. I was not alone any longer.

I swallowed hard as I opened the front door and slipped inside – a dirty, scared, untidy little girl, clasping my hands tightly together in the hall. I had no idea what I was going to say to my aunt; only to myself I kept whispering the words, "Even if I'm punished, help me to be good."

Then my aunt suddenly appeared at the kitchen door. We both stood looking at each other in silence.

But the loving Shepherd had found me, and when we first come to know his love he begins to make us more loving, too. As I stood stiffly in the hall something happened to my hard little heart that I had not expected. I suddenly ran forward and flung myself into my aunt's arms.

"I'm so sorry, Auntie," I whispered, "I will try to be good. And please, please don't send me away to boarding school. I want to stay here with you, and I'll never, never run away or be naughty again."

My aunt, kneeling in the passage, pressed my tear-stained cheek against hers and held me close to her. Then she smoothed back my tangled hair and kissed me.

"Oh, Ruth," she whispered, "I don't want to send you away if I can possibly help it. We'll try again."

Then she took my hand and led me to the table in the kitchen, where I sat down and ate a whole second breakfast to make up for missing my supper the night before.

Chapter Ten

My sheep hear my voice

I caught a bad cold from sleeping in the church, and had to go to bed for three days. Philip stayed with me most of the time, so we put in a lot of work on the bird book. When we were tired of drawing and writing we lay and talked. He was never tired of hearing about my night in the church, and I was quite pleased and surprised to hear how much everybody had missed me.

"I don't think auntie or uncle went to bed all night," Philip told me. "I couldn't go to sleep either. I thought you might be dead, and I was crying and crying in bed; then I went downstairs and I found Auntie crying a little bit in the kitchen. We had a lovely drink of hot chocolate together, and she gave me a chocolate biscuit, and we sat by the fire and talked."

"What did you talk about?" I said, hoping it had been about me.

"Oh, lots of things," answered my brother cheerfully. "I said perhaps you'd been drowned in Whippet brook. Auntie said she thought you were probably just hiding, and she might send you to boarding school as a punishment, and I said I thought it was a jolly bad idea."

"Why?" I asked hopefully.

"Because I shouldn't have anyone to play with on Saturdays," he explained. "I said I thought it wouldn't be any use, because you would run away at once."

"And what did she say then?"

"She said you wouldn't be able to. So I said it would be a pity to send you to boarding school, in any case, because I should probably have a nervous breakdown."

"Whatever's that?" I asked, with great interest.

"Oh, it's an illness you get when people do things you don't like. I heard Auntie talking about someone who had a nervous breakdown because the cook went away. So I said I would have one if you went away."

"Like measles?" I asked. Measles was the only illness I had ever had, and I thought it was very important.

"Oh, I don't know," answered Philip. "I don't think it has spots, but it doesn't matter, anyhow. You're not going now, but you'll have to be very careful about being good, because once she's thought of it she may think of it again."

I was silent. I hadn't told anyone yet about what had happened in the wood, for somehow I did not know how to put it into words. How could I make Philip believe that something had really happened? There was nothing to show for it, and sometimes, lying there with a sore throat and a blocked-up nose, I began to wonder how much of it was true, or whether perhaps I'd imagined it. And then I would take out my precious picture and look at it until I was sure again, when I would bury my face in the pillow and ask the Good Shepherd to let me feel close to him again, as I had felt that morning when we had walked home.

There was my Bible, too. As soon as I got home, I found it in the drawer and started to read it. After much searching, I found the chapter Mr Tandy had read to me about the sheep that was lost. I read it over to myself again and again until I almost knew it by heart. I read the rest of the chapter, too, about the boy who ran away, just like me, and who came home again and said he was sorry, and was forgiven by his father. I thought it was exactly like me and Aunt Margaret. I liked it very much indeed.

I tried to pray, too. I had been taught to say my prayers, but somehow it was different now. Before, it was just saying words because I thought I should do, but now it was talking to someone I knew and who loved me.

It was on my second night in bed that I made a great discovery. Philip had gone down to supper, and I had pulled out my Bible from under my pillow, for I was rather shy about letting anyone see me read it. As I turned the pages of the Gospels, looking for stories, I came across the tenth chapter of St John's Gospel, and the word "Shepherd" caught my eye at once.

I had often heard the chapter read in church and at school, but I had forgotten whereabouts in the Bible it came. Now I read it with great excitement. Here it was, all over again:

"I am the Good Shepherd: the Good Shepherd gives his life for the sheep."

I did not understand the verses about thieves and robbers, but I understood about the sheep following; that meant being good and doing what the Shepherd said – but what could it mean about "hearing the Shepherd's voice"? The clergyman had said that Jesus would speak to me, and that I must obey, but although I had lain in bed with my eyes shut, listening hard, I could hear nothing. How could I know his voice if he never spoke to me?

This question troubled me quite a lot that night and next day, until I suddenly had a good idea. I would go and see Mr Tandy, take him my postcard and tell him about what had happened. Perhaps he would be able to tell me about the Shepherd's voice.

I was very impatient to get up after this, and was allowed to go down to tea on the fourth day. It was a happy meal, and I went to bed thinking that after all it was much nicer being good. Being naughty was not really worth it.

Luckily the next day was sunny, and after dinner I set off joyfully across the fields with Philip. It was a special afternoon because I had not been out for four whole days, and also it felt rather precious because the end of the holidays was so near. We had a wonderful afternoon playing with a baby squirrel which Philip found in an oak tree.

Suddenly I thought of something.

"Philip," I said, "I'm going home now. You see, I specially want to visit somebody on the way back."

"All right," answered Philip happily, "we'll go. Who do you want to visit?"

"Mr Tandy, the shepherd," I replied.

"Good!" agreed Philip. "I like Mr Tandy; I'll come with you."

I stopped suddenly, wondering how I could explain. Philip just walked on, watching a magpie.

"Philip," I said slowly, "you can't come with me. You see, it's a secret, and I want to see Mr Tandy alone. It's something you don't know about, and I've got to go by myself."

It was Philip's turn to stop and stare now. He turned right round and looked as if he thought he had had heard wrongly.

"But why?" he asked at last. "You always tell me your secrets. I always tell you mine. You shouldn't tell Mr Tandy before me; I'm your brother, and he's only an old man."

I could see he was upset, and I felt dreadful.

There was a long pause, and I did not know what to say.

"Oh, all right," he said at last, trying to speak as if he didn't care. "I'll go on home. You'll find me in the orchard when you come."

He turned and went on, and I followed rather miserably. We walked single file in silence as far as the stile where the path split into two; one way led over the meadow towards home and one led up to the sheep folds.

"Good-bye," said Philip without looking round. "See you later."

He walked slowly across the field with his hands in his pockets. He must have been very miserable indeed, for he was not even watching the sky for birds.

And as I stood staring after his lonely little figure, I saw all in a flash – perhaps for the first time – what sort of a brother Philip had been to me. I remembered how seriously he had listened when I talked to him, how patiently he had joined in with my make-believe stories with my dolls; how quickly he would run back from school in case I should be missing him; and how faithfully he had stood by me when I was cross and bad-tempered and punished! As I thought of all these things, I suddenly didn't want to have any secret at all that I could not share with Philip. Of course, I wanted to go on belonging to the Good Shepherd, but not by myself. Philip must belong, too, and then we could enjoy the secret together.

I ran down the hill as fast as my legs would carry me, shouting his name at the top of my voice. He turned round and waited for me, and even as I ran I could not help thinking how much nicer he was than me – I would have walked off in a bad mood and pretended not to hear.

I was quite out of breath when I reached him, and sort of fell against him to stop myself.

"Philip!" I gasped. "I didn't mean it at all. I don't want to have secrets without you, and I'll tell you everything always, only you see there's a bit I don't understand and I can't tell you properly until I've asked Mr Tandy; but then I shall know all about it and I'll tell you in the wigwam tomorrow and you can have it, too."

The shadow passed at once from Philip's eyes, and his smile shone out again.

"It's all right," he assured me. "I don't mind you going to tell Mr Tandy, as long as you tell me afterwards. But it will spoil everything if we don't tell each other all our secrets."

I was so pleased to see him happy again that I flung my arms round his neck and kissed him. I had not done such a thing for a long time, and he looked a bit breathless and astonished, and glanced round the field to see that no one was looking.

I turned and ran back up the hill, but when I had gone half-way up I turned to look at Philip. He had his head thrown far back, watching birds. He had forgotten all about the quarrel.

I was very red in the face when I reached the sheepfolds, because I had climbed the hill so fast. To my great relief, Mr Tandy was there mending the gate. I ran straight over to him.

"Mr Tandy," I said at once, "I've come to tell you something. I've found out all about that story you read me, and I know that it means me, and that the Good Shepherd means Jesus."

He stood there with his hammer in his hand, looking down at me, with a look of real joy on his face.

"I'm really glad to hear it, little maid," he said. "Maybe you'll tell me a bit more about it."

"Oh, yes," I replied, pulling him down beside me on the seat. I was so pleased to find someone who would believe me that I forgot to be shy. I told him everything – about running away, and Mr Robinson and the picture and me belonging to the Shepherd.

Mr Tandy listened carefully, and his wrinkled old face was bright with happiness.

"Thank God for that, Ruth!" he replied, "For if you belong to him now, you'll belong to him for ever. No one can take you away from him."

"Mr Tandy," I asked, "are you one of his sheep?"

"Sure," he answered, "I've been one of his sheep for almost fifty years."

"Then, Mr Tandy," I went on eagerly, "have you ever heard his voice? It says his sheep hear his voice, but I've listened and listened, and he never says anything to me, and I do want to hear him so badly."

He thought for a long time before answering that question. Then he spoke very slowly.

"I'm going to call my sheep, Ruth," he said. "And when I call, take a look at them all, but you specially notice those over by the hedge, and see the difference."

I watched, fascinated, while he gave a low, clear call; every sheep in the meadow lifted its head and came a step or two nearer, except for the group by the hedge. They went on feeding quietly as though nothing had happened.

"Why don't they answer?" I asked. "Can't they hear you?"

"They can hear me well enough," answered the old man, "but they don't know my voice from all the others because they belonged to another shepherd who has been taken ill; they only joined my flock two days ago. But let them walk to the pastures with me for a week or two, and let me put them in my fold, and put my hands on their heads, and feed them, and they'll soon come to know my voice the same as the rest. Now, there are many voices speaking to your heart, Ruth, and you've only belonged to the Shepherd for a few days, so maybe you haven't learned to pick out his voice from all those others – for it's only a still, small voice."

"Then tell me how I can start," I begged.

"Well, it's like this," he said at last, after another long pause, "do you ever want to be a bad little girl?"

"Oh yes, often," I replied. "Before I ran away, I used to lose my temper and be rude to Aunt Margaret nearly every day."

"Well then," went on Mr Tandy, "you listen to this. Next time you want to lose your temper, you remember there's two voices speaking to you. There's the voice of the enemy telling you to kick up a row and stamp your foot and all the rest of it. But if you hold back a minute and listen, maybe you'll hear another voice – a little, quiet-like voice – telling you to be gentle and to do as you're told, and that's the voice of the Shepherd. And if you learn to take notice of that voice, he'll speak again, and you'll find you're hearing him all the time and everywhere. He talks to me out in these fields, and when I read my Bible he comes to me, and I know it isn't just a book of black and white print for clever people, but it's the voice of my Shepherd speaking to me."

Drawn by his gentle voice, the sheep had come quite close and were standing near his knees, their gentle faces turned up towards him. When he stopped speaking they moved away, cropping the grass.

I got to my feet and held out my hand. "Thank you very much, Mr Tandy," I said. "I'm going home now to listen, and I hope I shall soon want to get into a temper."

He shook his head. "Don't you wish any such thing!" he warned me. "And don't you try it alone. Remember, it is only the Good Shepherd who can stop you from doing wrong."

Philip was not in the orchard, so I went to look for him indoors. Rather to my dismay, I heard voices in the dining-room. They had already started tea, and I was late. We were not allowed to be late for tea, so I stepped into the room rather guiltily and made for my seat with a worried glance at Aunt Margaret. She was looking extremely cross.

"Ruth," she said sharply, "you're late again and I'm not going to have it. Sit down and eat your tea in silence – and you're not to have a chocolate biscuit."

Now this was a dreadful punishment, because I loved chocolate biscuits, and we hardly ever had them. I gave a little stamp with my foot and threw back my head. All my happiness disappeared and a great rush of angry words seemed to come springing up out of my heart all ready to tumble out of my mouth. In fact, I had actually opened my mouth, when I suddenly remembered!

If I got in a rage now, I wouldn't be able to listen to the little quiet voice of the Good Shepherd, and if I didn't listen now perhaps he wouldn't speak to me again.

It was so difficult to stop those angry words coming out that I had to clap my hand over my mouth to keep them in. And so I stood in the middle of the room, listening, while my aunt and Philip stared at me in the greatest surprise.

"What is the matter?" asked my aunt, coldly. "Have you bitten your tongue?"

Following the Shepherd meant being like him; if I was going to be like him I must stop stamping, shouting, answering back and sulking, because Jesus had never done any of those things. "Help me to follow you," I whispered in my heart, "stop me being angry, quick."

I drew a great big breath and put my hand back in my pocket; then I sat down in my chair without saying anything, for my anger was all going away. Auntie still continued to stare at me, but I went on munching my bread and butter in silence. I did not look at the chocolate biscuits, because I was afraid the sight of them might make me angry again.

We were all very quiet for the rest of tea, and when it was finished, Aunt Margaret said that as it was my first day up after my cold, I had better go straight to bed. I did not mind at all, for I had such a lot to think about that I wanted to be alone. I lay in bed with my arms thrown above my head on the pillow, looking at the stars and listening to the birds twittering till I fell asleep.

I was perfectly happy, because two wonderful things had happened that day for the very first time – I had heard the voice of the Good Shepherd, and I had kept my temper.

Chapter Eleven

The accident

We meant to go straight to the wigwam next day, and talk about the secret, but just as we climbed over the stile Terry popped up out of the ditch like a rabbit and said he'd come to spend the morning with us. We settled down on the bank to make plans.

As a matter of fact, Terry had already made all the plans, and we were just meant to follow them. He had found a high ash tree with a wood-pigeon's nest at the top, and if Philip wanted to see a wood-pigeon's egg he'd better come along right now because there were two beauties. It was an ash tree with a fork. Terry's plan was to collect some branches and bits of wood and make a sort of plat-form opposite where we could sit and watch the eggs hatch.

We were thrilled with the idea, and went scuttling off single-file through the wood. The tree Terry had told us about was quite a long way away, across the stream in the valley, and some way in among the larches that grew on the farther side.

It was well off the usual track, and the brambles and nettles grew thick around here. I followed the boys as best as I could, but even so my bare legs got dreadfully scratched and were as red as unripe blackberries when I finally caught them up. I sat down on the tree root and began mopping up the scratches with my handkerchief.

"Sorry," said Philip, "I forgot your legs were shorter than ours for jumping. If you keep up on the way home, I'll tread the brambles down for you."

Terry stared at my bleeding knees. "She's a brave little kid, ain't she?" he said, and I felt as if I'd been awarded a medal. I would willingly have walked through brambles and nettles to have earned such praise.

Terry had no time to waste. He crouched like a small panther and then leapt for the nearest branch of the ash. He caught hold with one hand and dragged himself up, the muscles rippling all over his tight little body.

"Now," he yelled, lying across the branch, "help Ruth up and I'll catch hold!"

Philip heaved me up on his shoulders, and Terry seized my wrists and pulled until I was able to clutch the branch; I gave a great wriggle, more or less turned myself inside out, and arrived panting beside him. Philip gave two great leaps, but fell backwards. On the third jump he caught hold of the branch and dragged himself up too. So we sat dangling our legs, like three happy monkeys, and we shared our biscuits with Terry, who always took it for granted that my aunt put in some for him too, and always ate much more than his share. But we didn't really mind, for we had decided long ago that Terry's mother must have starved him at home, as no one but a starving child could eat so hungrily, just like a wolf.

"Come on," said Terry, gulping down the last mouthful, "we'll nip up and take a look at her."

Off he went like a sailor on a rope, while Philip and I followed more slowly. The nest was on a sort of platform of twigs woven together, and as we got nearer to it we could hear the nervous murmur of the pigeon deep in her throat, then suddenly there was a whirr of beautiful pearl-grey wings and the bird flew up and settled on the topmost twig of the opposite fork, where she sat looking down at us and her nest.

It was such an untidy nest that I wondered how it was that the eggs didn't roll out – just a few loose-ly-woven sticks with some moss stuffed in the holes. But the eggs were burning hot and well cared-for, and the mother was very worried about them. Terry leaned back and stared at her.

"Nice spot to watch them eggs from," he remarked coolly. "I'm going up there myself."

"You couldn't!" protested Philip. "The branches wouldn't hold you; why, they'll hardly hold up the pigeon."

But Terry was rather a boastful boy. If anyone said you couldn't do anything, he immediately had to do it to show that he could. So now he just said,

"Go on – I'll show you," and swung himself across to the opposite fork.

Philip and I watched in fascinated silence as the thin, agile little boy climbed higher and higher. The pigeon saw him coming, flew up softly, and landed back with half-spread wings on her nest. We could only watch Terry. We had seen him do such daring and almost impossible things before, but this beat them all. Already the thin grey branches were bending outwards under his weight.

"Stop!" called Philip, in a rather husky voice; but Terry took no notice. Instead his laugh came ringing back to us through the leaves, and still he climbed – only he was climbing very carefully now.

"He's got there!" breathed Philip, and indeed he had. He was standing right out against the sky, clinging to a weak branch. The wind that moved lazily over the tree-tops had caught his hair and blown it back from his face, and his dark starry eyes were alight with laughter and triumph. When I think of Terry now, that is how I like to remember him, because it was the last time that we, or anyone else, ever saw him well and strong.

I can hardly write of what happened next. Philip and I have never spoken of it to each other, and I know we both never try to think of it, although I shall remember it all my life. We kept begging Terry to come down, but he took no notice of us and began to swing to and fro. Twice the branch bowed with him, but the third time it snapped. Terry was flung outward into space.

He gave one shrill scream that shattered the silence of the summer woods and haunted me in the night for many weeks to come. Then we heard his light body crashing through the leaves and twigs, which mercifully partly broke his fall; then came a sickening thud – and then silence.

I don't know to this day how Philip and I escaped falling after him and breaking our necks – we swung down that tree at such a speed. Even so, Philip reached the bottom long before I did, but I got there somehow and dropped onto the ground, gasping and sobbing, and lay trembling in a heap with my face hidden in the moss. I dared not look at Terry.

But Philip went down on his knees beside him, and had come to the conclusion that Terry was still breathing. He came over to me at last and put his arm around me.

"Ruth," he said, in a voice that was shaky and fearful, "I'm not quite sure, but I think he's alive. We can't possibly carry him. We shall have to fetch some men and a doctor, and I think I'd better go, because I can run much faster than you and I'm not crying so much. But, Ruth, we can't leave him alone, because he might wake up and be frightened and want someone. So would you mind staying with him, and I'll come back as quick as I can?"

I shuddered and shook my head violently; I couldn't be left alone – I was much too frightened. I clung to Philip sobbing, and begged him to let me go instead; but Philip wouldn't hear of it.

"You see, Ruth," he explained urgently, "he may die very soon, and if the doctor came in time he might be able to do something to make him better. I shall get there much quicker because my legs are so much longer. You must let me go at once, and try and be brave and stop crying."

He freed himself from my grasp, gently enough, and made off like the wind. I lay and listened to his footsteps crackling over the dead leaves and twigs, until the sound died away and only the murmuring of the pigeons broke the silence of the woods.

Now that I was left alone, I realised that I must make myself look at Terry. So I clenched my teeth and my fists and sat up.

What I actually saw was a great relief to me. I had never seen anyone badly hurt or unconscious before, and I had imagined that it would be a very horrible sight, but Terry, lying on his back with his arms spread wide, might have been asleep, except that his lips were too pale, and he breathed so lightly. He did not look hurt or frightened – only strangely peaceful, and as I sat there staring at him I began to start feeling strangely peaceful myself – as though he must soon wake up refreshed by such deep sleep and we should all be happy again.

The minutes seemed like hours and Terry did not move. Still I sat watching and wondering. Perhaps Terry was already dead – the thought made me feel cold and sick, and once again my eyes filled with frightened tears. If only Philip would come back! What was death, anyway? And if Terry were dead, where had he gone? We should bury his quiet little body under the ground in the churchyard, but I knew that that was not really Terry. Terry, I supposed, had gone to Heaven, like we sang about in hymns in church, but would Terry be happy? One grubby, rather naughty little boy, amongst all those golden streets and white wings!

Then I suddenly remembered Jane Collins, who had gone "to be with the Lord" – and the joyful face of the child in my dream. Perhaps dying just meant going to live with the Good Shepherd – hearing him speak with our proper ears and seeing him with real eyes, instead of just inside our hearts. That would be lovely, I thought; no wonder the little girl had looked so happy; and perhaps that was why Terry had looked so peaceful.

But Terry did not know about the Good Shepherd, so perhaps he might not be so pleased to go and live with him. I was sure Terry had never heard anything about it. If only I'd had a chance to tell him! If he didn't die, I should tell him at once, and then Philip and he and I would all belong together. But anyhow, even if he were dead, I was sure that the Good Shepherd would see that he was happy. Because, after all, it wasn't Terry's fault that he had never asked to be found and forgiven – it was really mine, because I had kept the secret to myself instead of sharing it.

So I sat hugging my knees, with my eyes fixed on Terry's still face, torn between hope and fear. Every few minutes I thought I heard Philip coming back, but each time it turned out to be only a rabbit, or a bird, or a gust of wind in the trees. The sunshine streamed through the thin bright leaves of the larch trees and rested in a bright patch on Terry's hair; almost as though God was touching him, I thought to myself; and I remembered how in the Gospel of Luke, which I read every morning, Jesus had touched men and women and children who were hurt or ill, and they always got well again at once.

"Oh God," I whispered, looking up through the branches, "please make Terry better – don't let him die – we want him here so much. Amen."

It was then that I heard Philip's voice through the trees and some men's voices talking, too; a moment later a little procession came into sight with Philip leading the way; behind him came Uncle Peter, who was always at home on Saturdays, and kind Doctor Paterson who had come to see me when I had measles; behind them came two men in dark uniforms carrying a stretcher; I heard later that these were the ambulance men.

Dr Paterson knelt down at once and put his fingers on Terry's brown wrist; he held it for a long time and then passed his hands over Terry's head, drew back his eyelids, and bent his legs and arms backwards and forwards very gently. Then he turned to me;

"Has the boy moved since he fell?" he asked.

"No," I answered, "he's been as though he was fast asleep all the time." Then I gave his coat a little tug. "Is he dead?" I whispered.

Dr Paterson put his arm around my shoulder. "No," he answered gently, "he's not dead, but he's very badly hurt. You were a good girl to stay here and look after him. Now we'll take him along to the hospital as soon as we can, and I'm going to see what I can do for him."

Very gently and carefully Terry was lifted on to the stretcher, and the men set off through the brambles with the precious burden between them. Uncle Peter, seeing how white and scared I looked, stooped down and picked me up in his arms like a baby; I snuggled up against him, and laid my head on his shoulder, and felt greatly comforted. I had always been good friends with Uncle Peter.

But I noticed Philip's face only when he glanced towards me, for he had walked with his head turned sideways; he said nothing, but his lips were pressed tightly together and his eyes looked very upset. His cheeks high up were scarlet, but the rest of his face was quite white. I longed to run and comfort him, but knew there was nothing I could say or do. Nothing would comfort him except Terry getting well.

We all walked very slowly so as not to jolt the stretcher, for the ground was rough and uneven. When we reached the road the ambulance was waiting there, and Dr Paterson climbed in with Terry while the men sat in front.

"When will you tell us if he's better?" I asked, just as he was about to shut the door.

"I shall be passing your house tomorrow," said the doctor, "and I'll drop in and let you know."

The door was shut and the engine started up; the ambulance sped off in a cloud of white dust and Uncle Peter, Philip and I were left to trudge home. Uncle asked us a few questions about Terry on the way, but otherwise we were very silent; nobody felt like talking.

It was a long, wretched day; we hung about the garden unable to settle down to anything, and with no appetite for our meals. Aunt Margaret felt sorry for us and read aloud to us after tea, but we were both glad when bedtime arrived. She came upstairs and kissed us goodnight, but as soon as her footsteps had died away I hopped out of bed and ran over to Philip. He was lying huddled up in bed, and I think he had been crying, for his voice sounded sniffy and his pillow was damp. I got under the rug at the bottom and curled myself up in a ball like a kitten.

"Ruth," whispered Philip, rather shakily, "do you think he'll die?"

"No," I answered firmly, "I don't."

"Why not?" enquired Philip, rather surprised at me being so sure of myself. "Did Dr Paterson say anything to you when I wasn't listening?"

I wriggled my bare toes up and down under the rug, as I always did when I was shy. It was difficult to explain, but I thought now was the moment to try and tell.

"Well, you see," I answered, "when you'd gone to get the others, I prayed to God very hard that Terry would get better again, so I expect he will."

Philip stared at me over the top of the sheet.

"So did I," he admitted slowly. "I said 'Oh God, please don't let Terry die' all the way home, but I don't know whether it was much use. I'm not a very good boy and I usually forget to say my prayers altogether, and nothing much happens when I do."

"But Philip," I said, uncurling myself and sitting up straight because I was so serious about this, "you don't have to be a specially good person to say your prayers; you just have to belong to the Good Shepherd. That's what my secret was, that I was going to tell you about today. I didn't make it up; the clergyman told me when I ran away, and it's in the Bible, too.

"When we're naughty, we're like sheep that run away and get lost and can't find the way back. But Jesus is the Shepherd; he comes to look for us, and

90

when we ask him he finds us – but he always waits till we ask. Then we belong to him and he listens to everything we say, and he speaks to us back and tells us how to be good. Mr Tandy told me that bit, and he spoke to me last night and stopped me from losing my temper with Aunt Margaret, when she wouldn't let me have a chocolate biscuit."

I could see Philip staring at me, his face pale in the moonlight. "Go on," he said.

"There's not much more to say," I went on, "except that when Terry was lying on the ground the sun suddenly shone through the trees right on to his hair, and I thought perhaps it was God's way of touching him and making him better, like Jesus touched people in the Bible. And after that I was almost sure he wasn't going to die."

There was a long silence, broken at last by Philip.

"Did you ask him to find you?" he asked, curiously.

I nodded. "I did it on the way home," I said, "in the primrose woods, under a tree. I asked him to forgive me for being naughty, and to find me and make me one of his lambs as the clergyman said – and oh, Philip, I wish you would come with me and see that clergyman, because he'd tell you about it much better than me, and I do so want you to belong to the Shepherd too."

"I wish I did," said Philip in a rather serious voice. "Do you think I could?"

"I'm sure you could," I answered, very firmly. "I should think you'd be much easier to find than me because you're so much gooder – I don't think you'd take much finding at all."

But Philip shook his head. "You don't know," he

said sadly. "You only see me outside. I'm not good at all inside."

"Well," I argued, "it doesn't matter. I'll show you my picture and you'll see; the sheep there is nearly falling over a precipice, he's got so lost, but the Shepherd is just going to find him all the same."

I tiptoed across the passage and returned with my precious picture in my hand. We both went over to the window and could see it quite clearly because the full moon was shining right in at the window. Philip went on looking at it for a long time.

"Could I ask now, Ruth?" he said at last, rather worriedly.

I nodded.

"Then you must go away," he explained, "because I shall have to be alone – we'll talk more about it in the morning."

So I left him, with his elbows on the window-sill, looking at the hills. I snuggled into bed and stared up at the millions of stars and thought about everything that had happened until I fell asleep.

Chapter Twelve

A visit to the vicarage

The rest of the holidays passed too quickly because there was so much to do. The doctor came to see us next day, and as soon as we heard his car stop we flung ourselves out of the gate, and nearly knocked him over in our eagerness to hear the news.

"Steady!" exclaimed Dr Paterson, catching us both by the collar. "If you knock me out I shan't be able to tell you anything."

Terry was alive, he told us, but he had hurt his back and head very badly indeed and would be in hospital many weeks. His mother was with him nearly all the time now, but as soon as he was a little better he would probably be moved to another hospital – a special hospital for people with broken bones. We could not go and visit him because it was too far away, but we should probably be able to write to him in a few weeks' time.

This was quite enough to stop us worrying and make us happy again. Terry was alive and being looked after; he would certainly get better soon, we told ourselves, just as we had always got better in time from measles and colds and tummy aches. So we settled down to enjoy the last few days of the holidays as much as we could.

We decided that we must pay one last visit to each of our friends, so Philip went to call on the bird man, and was taken down to see a moorhen's nest, and I paid a visit to Mr Tandy in the sheep folds.

The last day of all we had decided to visit Mr Robinson, and we set out at about half past three, because I'm afraid we thought it would be rather nice to arrive about tea-time.

The village lay at the bottom of the hill, and we marched in at the vicarage gate very sure of a welcome. Mr Robinson was in his shirt sleeves mowing the lawn, and recognised me at once. He seemed delighted to see us both. He did not even ask us if we would stay to tea; he simply said, "you've both arrived just at the right moment."

We had a lovely tea. Mr and Mrs Robinson sat in deckchairs and we sat on a rug and ate a tremendous lot and then we both told Mr Robinson all about our special secret while Mrs Robinson went in to see to the twins. He was so pleased – his face looked just like Mr Tandy's when I told him. He then talked to us about the importance of reading our Bibles.

"We'll do it together," I said, eagerly; "I think it will be fun to choose the verses, don't you, Philip?"

At that moment Mrs Robinson appeared at the window, wearing an apron. "Twins' bedtime, Ruth," she called. "Do you want to come and watch?" I jumped up. "Will you excuse me, please, Mr Robinson?" I enquired, a little worriedly, for I did not want him to think I was being rude.

"Certainly," he replied. "You go and help Mum: she'll be glad of a helper; Philip and I will stay here a little longer, and do some more talking."

I ran across the lawn and into the vicarage. The twins were crawling about on the carpet while their mother collected their night things; they were ten months old and very lively, and I, who had never had anything to do with babies, thought I'd never seen anything so wonderful.

I spent a wonderful half-hour; once they were safely in the big bath, Mrs Robinson let me soap their plump little bodies and then pour the water all over them; then we sailed a yellow sponge duck, and the twins screamed with laughter and beat the water with their fat hands. I was allowed to sprinkle baby powder over them, and when they were safely in their night clothes I was given a soft little hair brush with which I brushed their hair up on end.

It was not till their mother was tucking them firmly into their cots that I noticed the picture that hung on the wall behind them; it was another picture of the Good Shepherd – but it was different from mine. This Shepherd was standing by a lake, at evening time, with his hands stretched out to bless the little lambs that stood beside him and lay asleep at his feet.

"Why," I cried joyfully, pointing up at it.

"I've got a Good Shepherd picture, too, but it's not like that – my sheep is on a precipice."

"I know your picture," answered Mrs. Robinson, "and I love it very much, and later I shall show it to the twins; but they are not old enough to understand anything about precipices yet. I like to think that all through the night, when I'm asleep, the Good Shepherd is looking after my babies for me; so I put that picture there to remind me, and whenever I look at it I remember they are certainly safe."

I stared at the twins. They had both fallen asleep instantly. Janet had curled herself up and had stuffed two fingers into her mouth; Robin lay on his back with his arms thrown out on the pillow, his cheeks all warm and pink. I nestled up to Mrs Robinson and looked up into her face. She was quite young, with pretty hair and sparkly eyes, and I thought secretly that I should like her to be my mother.

"Can I come again?" I whispered.

"Of course you can," she replied. "You can come the Saturday after next if your aunt will let you – I'll write and ask her. I expect you have a holiday on Saturday; we'll take them out in the pram, and then you can help me give them their supper and put them to bed. It's a great treat for me to have a nanny, and I can see that you're handy with babies."

I blushed with pride, and slipped my hand into hers. I couldn't exactly have Mrs Robinson for my mother, but perhaps in time I might become a sort of older sister to the twins.

I went back to the garden and found Mr Robinson and Philip still talking seriously. I wanted to get back and ask my aunt about Saturday week, and I was extra pleased when the vicar said that Philip could come too, and help him in the garden, and we'd all have tea together.

We got back in good time for supper, and I ran straight off to my aunt.

"Auntie," I cried, hopping about on one foot, "Mrs Robinson has invited me to tea with her on Saturday week – her and the babies – and I can push the pram and put them to bed. I can go, can't I? Do say yes!"

My aunt looked rather annoyed.

"Who is this Mrs Robinson, Ruth?" she asked, rather coldly. "You're not to visit people without asking me first, I have never heard of the lady."

"Oh, she's quite all right, Auntie," I assured her, anxiously. "She's a very nice lady indeed, a clergyman's wife at Fairways; she's going to write to you."

"I should hope so," said my aunt,"but I'm afraid the answer will have to be No this time, because Miss Montgomery called this afternoon to say that her little niece was coming to stay, and I said that you would go and play with her that afternoon. I'm sorry you should be disappointed, but perhaps this Mrs. Robinson will invite you another day. If she really is the wife of the vicar of Fairways, I don't mind you going; I have heard they are very nice people."

I flew into a rage at once.

"But Auntie," I stormed, "you know that I hate going to tea with Miss Montgomery; and I hate Juliana Montgomery – she's like a little white mouse. She doesn't know how to play anything nice, and we have to sit indoors and play dominoes, and I hate dominoes. Oh, please, Auntie, say I need-n't go – I told Mrs Robinson I could come!"

"Then you had no business to tell Mrs Robinson," replied my aunt, sharply. "I have never heard such nonsense! You are never to accept invi-tations without my permission – and stand still while you talk; you are making me quite dizzy."

But I'd thoroughly lost my temper by this time, and was nearly crying with disappointment.

"I won't go!" I shouted, "I shall go where I like – I told Mrs Robinson I'd come, and I shall jolly well go, and you won't stop me!"

My aunt took hold of my arm.

"Go straight to bed," she said, firmly. "Don't let me hear any more of this rudeness; I thought you were going to try and improve, but this does not look like improvement at all – off you go!"

I shook myself free and marched off with my head in the air.

"I don't care," I muttered over my shoulder – and slammed the door behind me as hard as I could.

But I did care – very much indeed! Almost before I'd reached the top of the stairs, I'd realised what I'd done, and by the time I crept into bed I thought my heart was breaking. I curled up in a ball, buried my face in the pillow, and sobbed and sobbed.

I had forgotten to listen to the voice of the Good Shepherd. Perhaps he would never speak to me again; perhaps he would stop loving me. Perhaps I should even stop belonging to him, and then there would be no one to help me to be good. Oh, why hadn't I waited and listened.

"Ruth, what is the matter? You mustn't cry like this!"

I had been sobbing so bitterly that I never heard my aunt come in; I turned round quickly and tried to stop crying, for I did not really want her to see how sorry I was; she was sitting by my bed, and she had a glass of milk and a plate of biscuits in her hand.

"What is the matter, Ruth?" she asked again, and her voice was rather worried, for she had never seen me cry like that before.

I tried to answer in my ordinary voice, but could not manage it. I buried my head afresh in the pillow and began crying again.

I did not want to tell her, but I suddenly thought that she may be able to answer my questions, and I wanted to know the answer so badly that blurted it all out.

"It's the Shepherd," I sobbed. "I lost my temper and perhaps I shan't belong to him any more. Oh, Auntie, do you think I shall be able to come back to him, if I'm good next time?"

I lifted my face in my eagerness to hear her answer, but she was staring at me as if I had lost my senses.

"What are you talking about, Ruth?" she asked, helplessly.

I dived for the chair and found my picture in my Bible: I pulled it out, and held it in front of her with a great sniff and a gulp.

"That," I answered. "You see, I was his sheep, but I forgot to listen, and perhaps he'll never speak to me again, because I lost my temper so badly. Do you think, Auntie, he'd forgive me just this once?"

My aunt was staring very hard at the picture, and she didn't speak for a long time.

"Who gave you this picture, Ruth?" she asked at last.

"Mr Robinson," I replied, "and he told me all about it – you do know the story, don't you, Auntie? Do you think he will, Auntie, if I never, never do it again."

She was still staring at the picture and the answer was a long time in coming.

"Auntie," I whispered impatiently, giving her arm a little shake. "Do you think he might."

"If you are really sorry for being naughty, and are determined to try and be different, I am quite sure God will forgive you. You had better ask him."

My aunt stayed with me while I had my milk and biscuits, but we said very little. When I had finished, she kissed me good-night, and left me very sleepy and quite comforted. Before I fell asleep I buried my face in the pillow again and said a prayer for forgiveness to the Good Shepherd, who I knew cared equally for lost lambs, sleeping babies, and bad little girls.

Chapter Thirteen

We get a letter

The summer term passed very quickly. Philip and I spent long happy evenings on the Common playing cricket. Early in the mornings we often climbed the hills to watch the larks spring up from the bracken and fly high up into the sunrise. We loved to lie silently on the tops of the hills in the early morning and then race home to breakfast.

The summer holidays had come round again before we heard from Terry. All the summer he had been in a children's hospital in Birmingham, and from time to time we got news of him from Dr Paterson. We wrote to him quite a lot and told him all about the woods, what flowers were coming out, and what birds we had seen, but he never answered. So it was a great surprise when the postman, meeting us at the gate one morning, handed us a letter addressed to us.

Nobody but Mum or Dad ever wrote to us, and this was certainly not their writing. It was larger, and shaky, and looked as though the writer was not very used to writing letters at all. Philip politely handed it to me to open and looked over my shoulder while I read.

"Dear Filip and Ruth," it said, "I am come home now but i has to stop in bed. Please come and see me from Terry, my adress is Willow Cottage, the Hollow, Tanglewoods."

We were so impatient to start that we could hardly eat our dinner, and we talked about it all the time. My aunt didn't seem too sure when we showed her the note, but said we could go all the same.

"I only hope it's a clean cottage. Don't stay too long, will you?"

As soon as dinner was over we raced to our rooms to hunt in our drawers, for we wanted to take Terry a present. I found a bar of chocolate and Philip found a catapult, so we wrapped them up in separate parcels and put them in our pockets. Then we rushed out of the front door and set off for Tanglewoods. Tanglewoods was such a little village that it was really quite difficult to tell when you got there. There was a shop which sold groceries and candles, cattle food and medicines and cough mixtures and had a Post Office in one corner. Farther on was a tiny church with some old tombstones falling backwards. But the real Tanglewoods consisted of scattered farms and cottages along the low hills, and barns and outhouses hidden among the hop-yards. No one knew where

Tanglewoods started or ended, so Terry's address took us some time to find.

We came through the woods, and down over the hill where the view in front reminded us of a patchwork quilt. Everywhere we looked we saw risings and hollows and little hills and valleys and we stood for a while trying to guess in which particular hollow Terry lived.

There was no one in sight, and we made for the nearest farm to ask the way. We found a woman churning milk in a cool stone dairy. She came to the door, and pointed farther down the valley.

"You'll be meaning that tumbledown place down Sheep's Hollow; there's a gipsy sort of woman lives there with a boy – she's been up begging a lot of times. Follow the track down through the gorse bushes, and then follow the brook – it leads right down into the hollow.

We thanked her and went on, and she stood staring after us curiously, as though she would have liked to know our business at Willow Cottage. But we did not want to be held back, and we hurried down the hill as fast as we could until we could see the cottage in the hollow lying just below us, with its broken chimney-pot and the holes in the roof where slates had blown off.

It was a dark little hollow that had once been part of a quarry, although the clematis had covered up the bare rocks and made a green curtain round its sides; the stream trickled through it in a stagnant, slimy ooze, and we wondered why anyone should have chosen to build a cottage in such a damp, cheerless spot, when there was all the open hillside to choose from. But we learned later from Terry that it had been built as a hut for storing dynamite for the quarry, and only later made into a house.

It looked so miserable and deserted, with its broken windows stuffed with rag and nettles growing round the door, that we hung back half-frightened. Surely Terry couldn't live here! But as we stood hesitating at the entrance of the hollow, the door opened and a woman appeared and stood staring back at us.

We knew that she was Terry's mother because of her great black eyes, but even so we felt afraid of her. She was a big, powerful woman with dark skin and black, untidy hair gathered back in her handkerchief; her face was hard and unhappy and she looked at us as if she disliked us.

Nobody spoke for a moment or two – then the woman broke the silence.

"Well," she asked, "what do you kids want here?"

We came forward slowly.

"Please," explained Philip, "Terry wrote us a letter to come and see him, so we came. Please, we're so glad that he's well enough to come home."

The woman's face did not look any happier.

"Are you the children who was with my Terry when he fell?" she asked, suspiciously.

"Yes," we answered, rather guiltily.

"You didn't ought to have let him done it," she muttered. "Still, he's been carrying on something awful about you two coming to see 'im, so you'd best come in."

She jerked the door back roughly and led the way inside; we followed, but I slipped my hand into Philip's and held it tight. The little room into which she entered was gloomy, hot, and airless, and there was a strange smell, too, that made me want to sneeze. There was only one little window and it was too high to see through it.

But a moment later we had forgotten all this, and had both run forward with a cry of welcome. For on the bed in a corner lay Terry, and we had not seen him for three and a half months.

Of course we knew it was Terry because we were expecting him; but otherwise I'm not sure if we should have recognised him, for he was so changed. He looked so small and weak and pale.

He did not smile at us, for his face had grown so sullen and unhappy that he looked as though he hardly knew how to smile; but he held out his hand and said that he was really pleased to see us, and he'd been looking out for us ever since morning.

We said just as seriously that we were very pleased to see him, and then there was a long silence because none of us could think of anything to say at all.

Philip broke it at last by asking how Terry had enjoyed hospital.

"Tweren't bad," Terry admitted, "but I got fed up with lying so still like, and nothing to look at but them streets. And here it's just as bad – nothing to look at but that there wall; the window is too high up to see out of, and if I could, there'd be nothing to see but the side of the hollow."

"But couldn't we carry your bed outside?" I asked, looking doubtfully at the heavy iron bedstead on which he lay.

He shook his head.

"Couldn't get it through the door without taking

it to pieces," he replied gloomily, "and you can't move me off it – me back hurts too bad."

"Haven't you any books?" we asked.

"I ain't much good at reading," he answered, "although maybe I'd enjoy them if they'd got pictures in. What I want to see is them hills and birds and animals, and things."

His voice shook a little, and his big eyes filled with tears. Poor, tired, cross little Terry! We both felt dreadfully sorry for him, and didn't know how to comfort him.

"I'll bring you all my bird books," said Philip, who was looking most upset. "We'll come ever so often and tell you what things are looking like, and then when we've gone you can shut your eyes and pretend you're seeing them. I'll tell you what Tanglewoods looks like now, when we came over the hills this afternoon. The hay is still lying out in the fields, and the willowherb patches are just beginning to turn woolly; the hops will soon be ripe and are beginning to smell when you go past the yards, and the apples in the orchard are beginning to turn rosy and weigh down the branches. Oh, and I think they will cut the harvests very soon because the wheat is ripe and the wind makes nice noises in it, and I saw Mr Lake getting out his tractor, and there are lots of flowers – we'll bring you some round next time, and some apples."

Terry seemed pleased; a faint pink tinge crept into his almost colourless cheeks.

"You going to the hop fields?" he asked sadly.

"We might," I answered, "if Auntie will let us – we could earn some money then, couldn't we, Philip? – to help with the camera."

I used to earn a lot of money down at the hop-yards," said Terry. "Enough to buy me a pair of winter boots. Mum will have to try and go this year, but she can't leave me long, and she's had to give up her work to stop and mind me."

We didn't find it difficult any more to find things to say – in fact we talked so much that we stayed much longer than we meant to, and were interrupted by Terry's mother coming in with his tea.

Terry's meal was a cup of very strong tea and a crust thinly spread with margarine, on a chipped old plate; it did not look at all appetising to me, but it reminded me of the chocolate I'd brought. It had begun to melt in my pocket, but it was still very nice, and Terry's eyes really gleamed when he saw it. We did not give him the catapult because it did not seem as though it would be any use – his arms looked too thin and white to aim with it.

"Terry," asked Philip just as we were leaving, "when are you going to be able to get up and play with us again?"

He did not answer for a minute, but the frightened, unhappy look came back into his eyes.

"Maybe never," he whispered. "They think I don't know, but down at the 'ospital I heard the doctor talking to the nurse, and he said, 'It's all up with him, poor little chap – I can't do nuffing for him.' And I think maybe that's why they let me mum take me home. They can't do nuffing more to make me better."

We were horrified to hear this, and once again we could think of nothing to say to comfort poor Terry. So we left him, rather sadly; but just as we were going out of the door he called after us:

"When are you coming again?"

"We can't come tomorrow," answered Philip, "because we've got to go to the dentist. But we'll come the day after and bring the bird books."

"For certain sure?" called Terry.

"For certain sure!" we called back.

Terry's mother was out in the hollow hanging up a torn little night-shirt on the clothes line. She gave us a sour glance, but did not speak. When we said good afternoon she only grunted.

"What a miserable woman!" I remarked, as we climbed the hollow. "I'm glad she's not my mother."

But on the whole we were very silent on the way home, because we were both feeling so sorry for Terry and we were both wondering what we could do to make his life happier. Nothing we could think of seemed much good, because nothing could make up for having to lie all day in a dark, stuffy room, staring at the wall, while the apples ripened and the harvest fields rustled outside.

And as I walked home that hazy summer day, I realised for the first time how thankful I ought to be for the things that I had always taken for granted. I had never thought about it before, but now I suddenly noticed my strong little arms and legs, and my warm, healthy body. I paused on the top of the hill and looked over the countryside, then for one glad moment my heart suddenly rose up in thankfulness to God because I had eyes to see, and ears to hear, and feet to run.

Chapter Fourteen

A moonlight adventure

We went to see Terry very often during the next few weeks, and I believe now that it was only our visits that kept him alive through those long dark days when he lay flat on his aching back, staring at the wall. Philip lent him all his most precious nature books, and we took him all the chocolate we had, and baskets of fruit from the orchard. We felt well rewarded every time by the look of pleasure on his white cheeks and the flicker of happiness that would light up his eyes. He never thanked us in words, and his mother still stared at us as though she hated us, but we knew nevertheless that Terry's waking hours were spent wondering if we would come, and that he lay from dinner-time onwards with his eyes fastened on the door and his ears straining for the sound of our footsteps.

We had told Aunt Margaret about him, and once or twice she had sent him little presents. Aunt Margaret and I were slowly getting to understand each other, and I no longer tried to avoid helping her in the mornings. At first I had done my jobs because I thought I ought to, but after a few days I found that housework was really quite fun, as long as I was doing my best and not trying to get out of it all the time. My aunt said nothing, but I knew she was pleased at the change, and gradually we grew fond of each other and I began to talk to her more freely, instead of keeping everything a secret from her.

Uncle Peter was interested in Terry, too, and once or twice he had taken the step-ladder to the orchard and picked the enormous rosy apples that grew right at the top of the tree against the sky, for us to take to him. They were the size of big grape-fruit and when they were polished up we could see our faces in their shiny skins. Terry loved them, and even his mother looked interested.

"Did yer pick those in your garden?" she asked suddenly one afternoon, as we placed one of them between his small white hands.

We quite jumped, for except for her first greeting it was the first time she had ever spoken to us. We turned smiling towards her, for we wanted her to come to like us as much as Terry did.

"Yes," I answered, "we've lots of trees full of big, shiny apples like these. We shall be picking them in about a week, and then we'll bring some more; but we picked these early because we thought Terry would like them."

She only grunted and turned away, but I could

not help feeling pleased she had spoken to us and admired our apples. I thought I would try and talk to her again another day.

The nights just then were very hot, and owing to the extra "Summer Time" it did not get dark until very late. Philip and I used to kick our bedclothes onto the floor and lie in our night things by the open windows trying to get cool; and often I got tired of lying alone, and would go and sit on his bed. We would talk until the cool darkness gathered round us and we felt ready for sleep.

It was on one of these hot, still nights, when the sky was still red with the last glow of sunset, that I tiptoed across the passage and found Philip with his head out of the window. I pushed him up a little and stuck my head out beside him. In the distance we could hear a sheep cry up among the rocks.

"I don't think I shall be able to go to sleep all night, Phil," I remarked. "It's such a beautiful night, I seem to want to look out of the window all the time. It's full moon, too – look, I can see it coming up behind that fir tree."

We watched it climb above the horizon, almost blood-red in colour; it seemed all tangled up in the black boughs of the fir tree, but it would soon steer clear and all the world would be flooded with soft silver light. I turned suddenly on Philip, my head full of moonlight madness.

"Phil!" I whispered excitedly. "Have you ever been out on the hills at night?"

"No," answered Philip, "I haven't – not proper night. Why?"

"Oh, Philip," I breathed, giving his arm a little

squeeze, "Let's go now, just out through the hedge and up above the quarry. It would be so beautiful – just you and me, and the big yellow moon. Come on, Phil!"

Philip hesitated. "Do you think it would be very naughty?" he asked. "After all, you know, we were going to try to be good these holidays."

"I know," I urged. "And we really have been rather good, too – at least, I've been cross with Aunt Margaret once or twice, but last holidays I was cross nearly every day. And it isn't really a bit naughty, either – after all, what's naughty in wanting to see the moon? It's not hurting anyone and it's not even being disobedient, because Aunt Margaret has never actually told us not to go out at night and look at the moon."

Philip thought this over for a minute or two. It seemed to make sense to him, for all he said was, "Are you going to dress properly?"

"Oh, no," I said, "I shan't bother – I shall tuck my nightie up and put on my jacket. You put on your best trousers, those long ones, over your pyjamas, and put on your jacket, too."

This was no sooner said than done, and looking rather lumpy down below, with our handkerchiefs stuffed into our mouths because we wanted to giggle, Philip and I tiptoed to the front door and turned the key. It creaked and grated alarmingly, but my uncle and aunt must have been very soundly asleep, for although we stood still for several moments, nothing happened.

We shut the door silently behind us and stepped out into the open. Then we both stopped and looked around, because the world seemed so strange and different, and the sky with its millions of stars looked so far away. I slipped my hand into Philip's as I always did when things seemed strange, and together we tiptoed through the shadowed orchard towards our gap. The shadows of the apple boughs looked so fierce and frightening that I almost ran back – only Philip, having made up his mind, kept going.

Out through the gap and up the stony track that led to the hills we went without a word – up the steps behind the clock tower, over the first group of grey rocks – and we were there, standing on the lower slopes by moonlight, with the silver world lying at our feet.

We climbed in silence until we reached the very top of the North Hill and stood by the little pile of stones that marked the summit. The wind came sweeping up the valleys, clean and pure; a sheep lifted its head at the sound of our footsteps and bleated – otherwise all was silent and we sat down on the stones to look.

There was such a tremendous lot to see in spite of the darkness. Behind there were the black shapes of the hills and in front of us stretched the plains dotted with points of light, and every river and pond gleamed silver in the moonlight.

But mostly we looked up because we both loved stars, and tonight they all shone clearly, right across the sky. We pointed them out to each other with eager fingers.

It felt wonderful to be up there alone with the stars, and we stayed quite a long time, until Philip remarked that he thought we'd better be getting back, as it would soon be morning and we should be so tired next day. Actually it was not quite as bad as that, for when we reached the bottom of the hill, the clock on the tower struck one – and nearly made us jump out of our skins.

We sang all the way down because we knew there was no one to hear us, and it was a relief to make a noise after being so quiet. We sang all the songs we could remember, jumping over the gorse bushes and leaping from one rock to the other like two mountain goats.

But when we got back to the stony track we suddenly felt tired and thought how nice it would be to cuddle down into bed and go to sleep.

"Now," said Philip, "we must creep very, very quietly."

We were right through the gap and well into the orchard when Philip suddenly stopped dead and dug his finger-nails into my arm. With the other hand he pointed, and as I followed his finger my heart seemed to turn right over, and I only just stopped myself from screaming.

A tall figure in a dark cloak was moving towards us through the trees, bowed under the weight of a sack.

She had not seen us, for we had come very quietly, and we stood hidden in the deep shadows of the apple trees; but the figure was making for the gap, and in a few minutes must pass right by where we stood. I think I should have fainted if it had not been for Philip, who seemed much less frightened than I was.

"It's a woman stealing apples," he breathed. "We ought to try and stop her. They're Auntie's apples and she's got a great big sackful."

I could not argue or tell him to stop, because I was much too scared to speak. But I clung tightly to Philip and was sort of dragged with him when he suddenly stepped out into the open to stop the thief, who was nearly upon us. The moonlight shone full on her face, and we recognised her in a flash. It was Terry's mother!

She gave a short, terrified shriek and dropped the sack, so that the apples rolled out and scattered in all directions. Then she cowered down in the grass, and covered her face with her cloak and began mumbling words very fast, almost as though she was saying her prayers. Neither Philip or I knew what to do, until she suddenly flung back her fierce, proud head and spoke to us.

"So you'd be spying on me even by night, would you?" she hissed, shaking her fist at us. "And now you'll be sending the police after me tomorrow and they'll take me from my poor dying boy. You with your fine food, and your grand clothing, you can't spare the price of a few apples for my laddie what's starving and cold – and him dying before my very eyes, and with me nothing to give him. Oh, Terry, Terry! They'll take me from you..." She hid her face in her cloak again and burst into bitter, loud weeping.

I looked at Philip, feeling more troubled than I had ever felt before. Philip was frowning, too, as though he was wondering what to do next. Presently, however, he made up his mind, for he suddenly squatted down in the grass beside the poor huddled-up figure, and tried to take her hands away from her face.

"We weren't spying on you," he said gently, "we

were only here by accident because we wanted to see the moon."

The woman had stopped sobbing, and was looking closely at Philip, with a gleam of hope in her wild eyes.

"Little gentleman," she answered in a trembling voice, taking hold of him, "listen to me! I swear before God I'll never come again. I know I'm a wicked woman and I shouldn't have come, but my Terry's dying, and the doctor he says to me, 'You get him extra milk and a warm blanket for winter, and you feed him up proper if you want to keep him a bit longer.' And my Terry, he's all that I've got."

She was kneeling in the grass, clasping her hands almost as though she was praying to us.

I wanted to tell her that of course we wouldn't tell, and she could have all the apples she wanted, because I felt so sorry for her, but Philip stopped me.

"We won't tell," he said slowly, "but if you really stop stealing. as you say, I can't see how you are going to get any money. And yet, of course, it is very wicked to steal. Won't anybody give you any money?"

She shook her head.

"If I asked for Benefit they'd only put Terry back in hospital where I couldn't get to him. They'd say our house isn't fit for a sick child to live in, which it isn't, but at least we're together. That's what we want."

She looked at us desperately, as though begging us to understand. Philip still seemed to be thinking hard.

"Listen!" he said at last, in his most serious voice, "I think I've got a sort of idea, but I can't tell you about it now. You go back to Terry, and we'll come and see you tomorrow when we've talked about it – and we've promised not to tell."

"God bless you, little lady and gentleman," whispered Terry's mother, "and forgive me for being a wicked woman."

She picked up her empty sack and was gone through the gap in the hedge before we had time to say good-night to her. We were left alone, gazing down at the scattered fruit.

"I wish we'd let her have them," I remarked.

"No," said Philip. "It's Uncle Peter's fruit and it would have been as bad as stealing ourselves if we'd given it to her. I've thought of something else, Ruth, but I'll tell you in the morning. I'm so tired, and I want to go back to bed."

I was very tired, too, so I didn't ask him any more questions. We crept upstairs and tumbled into bed. I was just falling asleep when Philip's head came round the door.

"How much is there in the money-box?" he whispered.

"One pound, seventeen shillings and fourpence," I murmured back sleepily, and the next moment I was deep in the land of dreams.

Chapter Fifteen

About giving

Of course we both overslept next morning and were wakened only by the ringing of the breakfast gong and the sound of my aunt's footsteps coming up to see what had happened to us. She was rather suspicious at the sight of us only just waking up.

"I believe you don't settle down properly at night," she remarked severely, "or you'd be awake at the proper time. I believe there's a lot of running about when you should be tucked up, and I won't have it. Once in bed, you're to stay in bed, or I shall have to start locking you in."

Philip and I looked at each other guiltily out of the corners of our eyes and hoped our aunt would not say any more on the subject. Fortunately she was very busy, so no more questions were asked.

I was simply longing for a good talk with Philip,

but felt that I had really been so naughty the night before that I had better try to be extra good today. So I went down to the kitchen and offered to help, and my aunt was only too pleased to accept. We chatted together in a friendly way while we worked, and I couldn't help thinking how nice it was to have Aunt Margaret talking to me almost as though I was grown up. She never used to do it, and I began to wonder why things were different now.

"I think it's all to do with the Good Shepherd," I thought to myself. "It really has been different since Philip and I began to know about him. I do believe he really is beginning to make me less cross and less lazy, and I do believe Aunt Margaret is getting nicer, too. Perhaps after we've been to see Terry this afternoon we could tell her more about him, and ask if she has a blanket to spare so he wouldn't be cold in the winter."

Aunt Margaret suddenly stuck her head out of the window. "Come along, Ruth!" she called. "Think what you're doing; you've been standing there doing nothing the last three or four minutes."

I turned very pink and went on with my work in a great hurry. But I was longing to finish and get to Philip and tell him about my plan.

"You can go now," said Aunt Margaret, taking off her apron. "You've been a great help this morning."

I scuttled upstairs two steps at a time and found Philip lying flat on his bed with all the money from his money-box spread out in front of him. I knelt down and we counted it together.

"One pound seventeen shillings and fourpence," said Philip thoughtfully, "and I saw a camera for two pounds two shillings. If we both saved our pocket money for the rest of the holidays, we could get it by the beginning of term." On the other hand, if we gave Terry ten shillings for extra milk, we could get it round about Christmas."

He gave a little sigh, and I knew he was thinking of the squirrels' dreys and the dormouse nests that we should find when autumn came, and the nests of harvest mice that turned up when the corn was cut. I knew how much he wanted that camera.

"Oh, but I don't think we need give ten shillings," I cried. "Seven shillings and sixpence would buy a lot of extra milk and I think we could ask Auntie if she's got an old rug."

Philip fingered his coins.

"Well," he said, "I don't think we really need decide now. We can think it out on the way. I'll take the whole money-box, and then if I want to give her seven shillings and sixpence I can, and if I decide more like ten shillings, I can too!"

I agreed it was too important a matter to decide in a hurry, and we packed the money back.

We set off after dinner to Terry's house. I carried my Bible with my picture tucked inside; Philip carried the money-box, which was very heavy and jingled as we walked; but he was rather quiet, and I thought he must be thinking of the camera and really wanting it, so I longed to cheer him up.

"Philip," I said, "I think five shillings might buy quite a lot of extra milk. Let's ask how much extra milk costs."

Philip only grunted; he didn't seem to want to talk about it at all, so we walked on in silence.

We were half-way down the hill towards the hollow when Terry's mother suddenly appeared from behind a tree, where she seemed to have been waiting for us. She looked at us with a very worried look on her face, as though we might have forgotten our promise.

"I thought we might have our talk out here," she began nervously, "before you go on down to Terry. You won't tell my Terry nothing about them apples, will you now? I did it for his sake, but he'd get really upset if he knew. He's a good lad, my Terry."

"Of course we won't tell Terry," said Philip. "We promised we wouldn't tell anyone. Let's talk here on the hill, and he won't be able to hear us."

We sat down among the flowers and were silent for a little while. Philip looked at me because he was expecting me to begin. I looked at the ground because I was shy, and Terry's mother looked very hard at the money-box.

"We've brought you some money to buy milk and bed-clothes for Terry," he said simply. "It's not much, but it's all we've got," and as he said it he tipped up the money-box and emptied the whole lot into Terry's mother's lap.

"It's one pound seventeen shillings and fourpence," he said clearly, so that there might be no mistake about it, "and we hope it will do Terry a lot of good. Now we will go down to the cottage and see him for a little bit."

He stood up and started off down the hill, but I stayed behind for a moment. The Good Shepherd had given his life; Philip had given all the money for his camera – and I wanted to give something, too. I suddenly remembered that my most precious possession was in my hands. So I opened my Bible and pulled it out and laid it with the coins in Terry's mother's lap.

"This is my favourite picture," I said softly. "And you can have it to remind you that Jesus, the Good Shepherd, wants to find you. Philip and I both belong to him now."

"Thank you, little lady," she replied, and I left her sitting there counting her coins on the hillside, while I ran after Philip.

"I hope you didn't mind that I gave her all the money," said Philip, as we were walking home an hour later. "After all, a lot of it was yours really, but somehow I felt we couldn't keep it – I mean the camera doesn't seem to matter much compared with Terry, when you come to think of it, does it?"

"No," I agreed, "and the funny part is, I was thinking the same thing. When I thought about the Good Shepherd giving his life, it seemed awful to be giving such a little, and I was trying to make you look at me – to tell you to give more."

"Funny," said Philip, "I thought I should feel miserable without my money, but actually I feel really happy."

"Yes!" I agreed. "I thought it would be terrible giving away my picture, but I sort of feel glad she's got it now. Isn't it strange?"

"We never guessed it would be so nice, said Philip but when you come to think of it, Ruth, I believe it's the first time we've given away anything that we really wanted to keep badly, so we couldn't have known."

And we walked on in silence, thinking about it.

Chapter Sixteen

Hops and mushrooms

The summer holidays were specially exciting that year, because my aunt gave us permission for the first time to spend some afternoons in the hop-fields, where we earned quite a lot of money. We had given up saving for the camera for the present, and our idea was to earn enough money to buy a warm blanket for Terry. We had told Aunt Margaret about it, and she had suggested it, as she hadn't actually got one to spare herself. But she gave us other little things for him, and mended up Philip's old pyjamas, which were thick and warm.

Mr Robinson had also promised to go and see Terry. On one of our many Saturday visits, Philip and I had told him about Terry and had begged him to call.

"You see," I explained, "I've tried to tell him

about the Good Shepherd, but he doesn't want to listen. He says if God loved him he'd make his back better and let him run about again, and when he said that, I didn't know what to say – but if you came, you could explain it all nicely, I expect, couldn't you?"

Mr Robinson had smiled.

"No," he answered, "I couldn't explain it at all, because when sad things happen in our lives he often doesn't tell us why. If we really love him we must believe what he says even if we don't understand. That is what 'trust' means. In any case, Terry would probably listen to you more than he would to me because you are a child like himself and I'm only a grown-up."

"But he doesn't listen," I had insisted. "He doesn't take any notice of me at all; he just tells me to talk about something else."

"Well, then," Mr Robinson had replied, "you must start praying every day that he will listen. God doesn't always answer our prayers at once, but he hears them, and if they are right prayers he always answers them in the end."

Philip and I loved the hopfields with the noisy pickers and the strange smell that clung to our clothes and fingers. At six o'clock we would line up for our pay and feel so important and grown-up when our money was handed out to us.

Once a family from Birmingham invited us to stay to supper with them, and we sat round a glowing fire. They cooked a strange sort of pancake in a big frying pan. It smelt delicious, and when it was tossed on a tin plate and handed to us we thought we had never tasted anything so good.

We found another way of earning money, too, which Aunt Margaret thought was better than hop-picking.

One misty September morning we got up early and ran out into the silver fields where the spiders were covering the grass with their webs. We took off our shoes and socks because we liked the feel of cold dew between our toes, and were skipping up and down the field, when Philip suddenly stopped. He had caught sight of a little white button mushroom and stooped down to look underneath and make sure it wasn't a puff ball.

"Mushrooms, Ruth!" he called. "Let's see if we can find some more!"

We found lots more – in fact, the field was full of them, big ones and little ones, and we heaped them up until we could have filled a whole basket, only we had no basket.

"There's only one thing to do," Philip remarked. "You must take off your vest and tie the sleeves in a knot so that it makes a bag. We must get these mushrooms home somehow."

When my vest had been filled up with mushrooms it began to stretch, and by the time we reached home it had grown so long that it almost touched the ground. We were going to give some to Aunt Margaret to cook and we were going to ask whether we might sell the rest to the greengrocer up the road.

Aunt Margaret was pleased with the mushrooms, but she was not at all pleased with my vest. She said it was enough to give me a bad chill, and it was ruining good underwear. So I was given a dose of medicine in case I should catch a cold and made to wash the vest, which made me sulky all breakfast time.

But I cheered up later, because when we asked Aunt Margaret if we might sell the rest of our mushrooms to Mr Daniels the greengrocer, she said she did not mind at all, as long as we took them in a proper basket. So we set out, highly excited, marched up to the counter, and asked to see Mr Daniels personally.

Mr Daniels was fat and bald, and wore horn-rimmed spectacles on the end of a large red nose. He liked Philip and me and beamed at us over the counter. When he saw our mushrooms he threw up his hands in admiration.

"Dearie me!" said Mr Daniels. "I'll weigh them out and pay you the same as I pay the farmers, and if you find any more, you bring them along to Mr Daniels."

We did find lots more, and by picking mushrooms and hops, the money-box began to get really heavy again, and we were beginning to talk about the colour of the blanket we would buy, when a wonderful thing happened.

We had wandered over the hills in the heat to take Terry some plums, and we found him alone. The house was more stuffy than usual, and Terry looked hot and flushed; his dark hair lay in damp locks on his forehead, and he had thrown all his bedclothes back. He did not notice us come in because he was staring so hard at the wall opposite, where his mother had hung the picture I had given her.

"Hello, Terry!" we greeted him, sitting ourselves down on the bed. "Is your mother out?"

"Mm," answered Terry, wearily. Poor Terry! He seemed so exhausted that even our arrival didn't cheer him up. "She's been gone a long time."

"Where to?" we asked.

"I don't know," replied Terry. "She wouldn't say."

There was a pause, then Terry spoke again in a fretful voice.

"Take that picture away with you!" he commanded. "It really bothers my mum. The last few days she's sort of cried when she's looked at it; she was happier before you brought it and we don't want it."

"But I can't take it away," I objected. "It's your mother's – I gave it to her; it would be sort of stealing to take it away."

Terry passed his hand wearily over his forehead and turned his face to the wall.

"I wish I was dead," he muttered.

We had never seen Terry quite so unhappy before, and we longed to comfort him; but what could we say to comfort a boy who had to lie in this hot, cheerless gloom all day long? Even when we offered him a a plum he pushed it away.

"I'm feeling sick," he explained. "Maybe I'll eat it later."

We left very soon, because he seemed too tired to want us. His mother had not returned, and we felt very depressed as we climbed the hill.

"Philip," I said, "do you still pray every day that Terry will get better?"

"Not every day," answered Philip, "because sometimes I feel sure he won't – I mean, perhaps God thinks he'd better not get better. The doctor said he wouldn't, you know, and doctors are usually right."

"But God could do a miracle," I insisted, "like he did in the Bible – it seems too awful, doesn't it? Terry seems sadder every time we go."

"It isn't really being ill that's the worst part," Philip said seriously, "it's that awful little house. It's so hot and dark, and there's a nasty smell about it, and it must be so dull and boring. If he could be ill somewhere nice it would be different."

But I could find no way out of this difficulty at all, unless we prayed that someone with a nice house would adopt Terry – and, when we thought about it a bit more, we decided not to pray for that after all, as Terry would hate to leave his mother and his mother would hate to lose him.

We were talking so seriously about it all when we reached the gate that we did not look where we were going and nearly bumped into Aunt Margaret, who was coming down the path talking to a tall woman in a dark cloak. We looked up quickly into the visitor's face, and to our utter astonishment we saw that the tall woman was Terry's mother, and her dark eyes were red with weeping. And, stranger still, my aunt was talking gently to her and had laid her hand on her arm.

They neither of them took any notice of us, and we went indoors quickly because we somehow felt that Terry's mother hadn't really wanted to meet us at all; but once inside we looked at each other in astonishment. What could Aunt Margaret and Terry's mother have been saying to each other?

"Perhaps she's asking for things for Terry," I suggested.

Philip shook his head.

"I don't think it's that," he said, "because Auntie was being so nice to her, and usually she's rather cross with beggars."

If we had hoped that my aunt would explain things, we were disappointed. She came back into the house a few minutes later and went upstairs to her bedroom. When she came down she was very quiet and took no notice of us at all. I thought her face was sadder than usual and she seemed to be thinking hard.

Next day at breakfast another surprise awaited us. Aunt Margaret laid down her knife and fork and looked at her watch.

"Ruth," she announced, "I am going out for the morning; it is very important and I shall probably not be back for some hours, so I am going to let you get the dinner. The potatoes are peeled, and there is cold meat, so you will only have to wash the lettuce, and peel and stew the apples and make some custard. I showed you how to make custard the other day, so it will be a good chance to try."

Philip and I stared at her in astonishment. Never before, that we could remember, had our aunt gone out for the morning, or missed cooking the dinner; it must have been very important business that called her, and we really wanted to know what it could be.

Aunt Margaret was as good as her word. She got up from the breakfast table, put on her hat, and walked straight out of the front door – and that was the last that we saw of her until dinner-time.

Philip and I, left by ourselves, went to work with a will. I really liked the idea of being mistress of the house for the morning, and we carried the breakfast things out and started to wash up, feeling very important. I began by tipping nearly a whole jar of soap flakes into the bowl and whisking until the foam stood up nearly as high as the taps – and after that, of course, we had to spend ten minutes or so scooping it up with our hands and blowing soap bubbles all over the kitchen.

The morning passed very happily. Philip and I peeled enough potatoes to feed an army, and although I burnt the saucepan badly while making the custard, it didn't taste much. We caught three little slugs in the lettuce and carried them carefully back to the lettuce patch in case their mothers should be missing them; then when we felt the dinner was prepared properly, we started on the housework. We took all the rugs into the garden and danced up and down with them, smothering ourselves with dust. Yes, it was certainly great fun being left in charge of the house. The morning went very fast and it seemed only a very short time before Aunt Margaret walked in at the gate. It was dinner-time.

I made a dive for the potatoes, which were boiling merrily, and the dinner was served up by a very flushed, untidy little cook, who had to be sent away from the table to brush her hair the minute Grace had been said.

However, my aunt seemed pleased with my efforts; she praised the potatoes and salad and said nothing about the burnt flavour of the custard. She looked happy, too; much happier than she had looked at breakfast, and now and then we noticed her smiling to herself as though she had some very nice secret.

"I hope you enjoyed this morning, Auntie," said Philip, politely.

Aunt Margaret's eyes twinkled, and a little smile turned up the corners of her mouth again.

"I've enjoyed myself very much indeed, thank you Philip," she replied seriously; then after a moment she added: "Tonight, when Uncle Peter comes home and I've talked to him, I'm going to tell you about it, but till then it's a secret."

Philip and I were very interested. When evening came we kept running out into the road to see if Uncle was coming. When at last we saw him approaching we dashed madly into the kitchen.

"He's coming, Auntie," we shouted; "now, the secret, the secret!"

She shooed us both out of the kitchen with a wooden spoon.

"Get along with you," she said. "I can't make fish cakes and talk secrets at the same time. You tell your uncle to come here, and then you run out into the garden."

So Uncle Peter went in and shut the door.

Chapter Seventeen

The secret

"Now for the secret!" we exclaimed, and settled ourselves really comfortably on the stools at my aunt's feet.

We were sitting in the early summer evening just outside the French windows. The air was sweet with the scent of roses, and bats fluttered past on restless wings. Aunt Margaret leaned forward in her chair while she talked, and as the story went on, we crept closer and closer until our heads were resting against her knees.

"Well," she said, "before we start talking about secrets, I want to know what you were doing in the orchard at one o'clock in the morning a few weeks ago?"

We both jumped and went very red; this was most unexpected. But strange to say, Auntie didn't sound particularly cross; in fact, there was a tiny shake in her voice that might have meant that she was trying not to laugh.

After a very uncomfortable silence, Philip answered in a small voice.

"We couldn't go to sleep that night," he explained, "and we wanted to see the stars close up. So we put some clothes on and went up to the top of the Hill and then..."

"You went up to the top of the North Hill, alone in the dark?" interrupted my aunt, sounding very shocked.

"You've never actually told us not to," I chimed in quickly.

"Ruth," said my aunt solemnly, "there are a great many things I have never actually told you not to do, but which you know in your heart I shouldn't like, so don't make silly excuses. Now before we go any further I want you to promise me that you will never go out alone again at night as long as you live with me."

We both promised most earnestly.

"Very well, then," continued my aunt. As long as you understand that, we will say no more about it. Now perhaps you are wondering how I came to know about it."

As a matter of fact, we thought we could guess, but we did not say so.

"Yesterday," said my aunt, "just after you had gone out, Terry's mother came to see me. She had a long story to tell me. She told me that some weeks ago she was in despair about earning some extra money to buy a blanket for her little boy, and when she saw those big rosy apples you took to Terry,

133

she decided to come at night and help herself. She did this once or twice, taking a few pounds from each tree so that your uncle wouldn't notice, and earned quite a lot of money by selling them to the greengrocers in the villages around Tanglewoods. Then one night she met you in the orchard."

We looked guiltily at each other and wondered whether my aunt would be very cross with us for not telling. We weren't enjoying this secret much!

"You promised not to tell," went on my aunt, "which wasn't very sensible of you, because if you had told me all about it sooner I might have been able to help her sooner, but still, I know you meant it kindly. And then she told me that you went to see her and took her all your money. And you, Ruth, gave her your picture and told her the story of the Good Shepherd."

I blushed again; I was rather shy about my picture.

There was a long silence and we sat quite still with upturned faces waiting for Aunt Margaret to go on.

"She came to see me and brought me the money from the apples she had stolen. She said she felt as though Jesus, the Good Shepherd, was calling her, and she could get no rest until she had answered him. And then we had a long talk and she told me all about that little boy of hers, who seems to be dying in that dark hovel of a home. I went to see him this morning and it's all true. She can't leave him to go to work, and she won't be parted from him to let him go back to hospital, and they are as near starving as one can be nowadays."

My aunt stared out into the twilight. She seemed to have almost forgotten us.

"And when she had gone last night, Philip and Ruth, I think the Good Shepherd spoke to me too. I have not thought about him much for a long time, but last night he showed me a lot of things."

My eyes were fixed on my aunt's face, and I had drawn so close that she put her arm around me.

"He showed me a great many things I can't tell you about now, but I will tell you about two of them. He showed me a lot of money lying doing nothing in the bank, and he showed me an empty room all covered up with dust-sheets, but with a beautiful window looking out over the plain with the sun shining in through it every morning, and the beech tree just outside."

I gave a little jump. "The best spare bedroom," I whispered.

My aunt nodded. "Yes," she agreed. "The best spare bedroom that's been empty for such a long time. But it's not going to be empty any longer, because we want to use it for the Good Shepherd. So the day after tomorrow, Terry and his mother are coming to live here with us for a time. Terry's mother is going to help me in the house, and Terry is going to lie by the window in the spare room and get some colour into his cheeks. It will be his very own room, and you and Philip shall help arrange it, and get it ready tomorrow. Would you like that?"

Should we like it? We were both so glad that we couldn't speak one word, but I think our faces must have shown our joy, for Aunt Margaret laughed a little and seemed to understand.

Philip's eyes anyway were quite starry with happiness.

So we sat and talked until the moon had risen high in the sky, then Uncle Peter came and stood in the doorway and we flung ourselves upon him.

"Do you know?" we shouted joyfully. "Do you know?"

"Of course he knows," said my aunt, laughing. "You don't think I'd turn the house into a hospital without asking him?"

So we were hustled off to bed, and were told we needn't even wash, except for faces and hands, because it was so late – which was certainly a perfect end to a perfect day.

We spent most of next day getting the room ready for Terry; we spring-cleaned it ourselves and made up the beds – one in the corner for Terry's mother and one by the window for Terry. We collected our nicest books and toys and arranged them where he could see them, and then hung up our brightest pictures on the walls. We picked the rosiest apples and the yellowest pears and put them in a dish by his bed; then we stood and looked round and decided that it was quite perfect.

Chapter Eighteen

Terry at home

Terry arrived in an ambulance, at teatime, and his mother came with him, carrying their few belongings in an old tin box. Aunt Margaret had arranged for the ambulance, and Terry had been lifted and carried as gently as possible, but even so he was tired out. When they had laid him in his bed by the open window and his dark eyes turned sadly to the beech tree, his small face looked as white as the pillow beneath him.

"It's smashing!" he whispered, with tears rolling down his cheeks.

The rest of the summer holidays passed quietly. Terry seemed perfectly happy, and would lie for hours looking out of his window with his arms thrown over his head. His mother cared for him tenderly and I thought how much nicer she looked when she was doing things for Terry – her whole face seemed to grow gentle.

While Philip spent his evenings at the dining-room table with his school-books spread out in front of him, I would sit upstairs with Terry. Sometimes I would read aloud to him, but sometimes I would perch on the bed, and leaning my elbows on the sill, I would stare out into the dusk and talk.

We talked about a great many things, for Terry, now that he was too ill to do much else, thought a good deal. We often went back to those happy days in the wigwam, and talked about nests and animals. Sometimes we talked about the accident, and about the hospital, and the long, dreary days in the dark hut; sometimes about my mother and father and how pleased they would be to see Terry when they came home.

"Ruth," said Terry suddenly, as we sat in the twilight one evening, "what's dying like?"

I shuffled my feet uneasily. "Oh, I don't know," I answered, "but I think it's very nice. At least, I think it's just like going to a beautiful place where Jesus is, and where everyone is happy. Why, Terry?"

"Because I heard the doctor in the hospital say it," said Terry, looking round to see that no one else was going to come in at the door. "I told you once. He said 'It's all up with him poor little chap!' – and that means dying."

"But that was a long time ago," I said.

He shrugged his thin shoulders.

"I ain't got no better," he replied. "Ruth, does everyone go there?"

"I'm not sure," I answered, slowly. "I think perhaps you have to ask the Shepherd to find you. I think you have to belong to him. But that is quite easy, Terry. You only have to ask to be found, like the sheep in the picture."

He frowned. "I was a bad boy," he admitted, doubtfully. "I pinched ever such a lot of things whenever I could lay hands on them. The cops nearly got me once."

"I think it would be all right, all the same," I assured him. "But, Terry, I'll ask Mr Robinson to come and see you. He could tell you about it ever so much better than me."

There was a pause; Terry didn't seem very happy at the thought of Mr Robinson coming to see him.

"Ruth," he said at last, "where's the picture – the one you gave us?"

"Oh, you mean my picture?" I answered. "I don't know, Terry; I suppose your mother's got it."

"I'd like to look at it again," he said. "I told Mum to take it away because it upset me to see that sheep stuck on the rocks and wondering whether maybe the Shepherd couldn't reach it. But as it's Jesus, I expect he could reach anywhere, couldn't he?"

"Oh, yes," I answered, feeling very sure of myself. "Jesus can reach anywhere; nobody could stray away so far that Jesus couldn't bring them back. Mr Robinson told me so, so you needn't worry about the sheep. It's quite all right."

"What I'd like," went on Terry rather dreamily, "would be a picture of that sheep after the Shepherd had picked him up – when he was safe in the Shepherd's arms and being carried home; I'd really like that."

"Would you, Terry?" I asked eagerly. "I'll try to get you one. I'll look everywhere and see what I can find."

Terry gave a sad little smile and seemed too tired to talk any more; so we sat in silence until his mother came up to settle him for the night, and I slipped downstairs to see whether Philip had finished his lessons.

I did not forget my promise to Terry, and on the first Saturday of the autumn term I set out to ask Mr Robinson's advice about the picture. Philip had stayed at school to play in a football match, so I had to go alone.

Mrs Robinson was sitting at the window sewing, so I stopped and had a chat and a chocolate biscuit with her. The twins were rolling about in the playpen, and I had a game with them, so when at last I reached the church where Mr Robinson was getting ready for the Sunday services it was quite late in the afternoon, so I told him straight away why I had come.

"Mr Robinson," I started, walking up the aisle very fast, "do you remember that picture you gave me?"

He stopped what he was doing and sat down on the steps; I sat beside him. It was one of the nice things about Mr Robinson – he always gave you his whole attention.

"Indeed, I remember it very well," he replied. "Because, as you know, I have the same one hanging in my room."

"Oh, yes," I answered, "Of course you have. But, Mr Robinson, I want to get the next picture to that one. Do you think it would be possible? Do you think there is such a picture?"

Mr. Robinson looked very puzzled.

"I'm afraid I don't understand what you mean by the next picture," he said gently. "Do you mean another picture by the same artist?"

"Oh, no," I answered. "I don't mind who's painted it – I mean a picture of what *happens* next, after the Shepherd has picked up the sheep, and when it's safe in his arms. You see, Terry doesn't like my picture. It makes him feel unhappy because he says he can never feel sure when he looks at it that the Shepherd will really be able to save that sheep. You see, the Shepherd's arms don't look very long and the sheep is a long way down the precipice, and sometimes it bothers Terry, so I thought I'd try and get him the next picture, where the sheep is safe, and where there's nothing more to worry about."

Mr Robinson's eyes had never left my face while I was speaking, and when he answered, his voice was very serious.

"I will try my very hardest to get Terry the next picture," he said. "But, Ruth, you mustn't let Terry think that about the sheep. Do you think you could teach him a verse from the Bible, if I taught it to you first?"

"Oh, yes," I answered, "I'm sure I could. I've taught him lots already. Is it a Shepherd verse?"

"Not exactly," said Mr Robinson. "At least, it doesn't actually mention the Shepherd, but it's about him, all the same. It's this: 'He is able to save completely those who come to God through him.' However far the sheep had strayed, however high it had climbed, however low it had fallen, the Shepherd could still reach it. It means that there are no people in the world, however naughty or however far away from God, whom Jesus cannot save as soon as they ask him."

I looked up quite satisfied. "Yes, I'll remember all that," I said, "and I'll tell Terry. Then he needn't worry about that sheep any longer. Thank you, Mr Robinson."

"And on Monday," my friend promised, as we left the church, "I am going over to Hereford and I will look in the shops and see if I can find the picture you want."

I told Terry all about it that night, and he was glad to learn the Bible verse. He promised to feel quite certain about the poor sheep getting safe home, because now he understood that even the worst precipice couldn't stop the Shepherd from finding that sheep.

But poor Terry was very tired that night – so tired that I only stayed a few minutes. His face looked even whiter than usual, and he kept screwing it up as though the pain was very bad. His mother had hardly left him all day, and Aunt Margaret had been cooking really nice things to try and get him to eat something, but it was all no good. Terry turned his face to the window and lay silent and uninterested.

Several days passed and the beech leaves outside began to fall rapidly; Terry hardly spoke, but he liked watching them whirling about, and although his mother sat beside him most of the time, he usually lay looking outside. The doctor came two or three times during the week, but each time he looked so sad and serious that I dared not ask him how Terry was getting on, and when he would be able to play again.

One afternoon I came running in from school to find that Philip was late. So, flinging down my school bag, I skipped upstairs and then opened Terry's door very softly, for during the past few days even I had come to realise that I must be quiet here.

But I stopped in amazement in the doorway, for beside the bed sat Mr Robinson, and Terry's thin face was turned towards him with a sort of smile on it, while he listened to a story about a tiger.

I pulled up a chair and listened, too, until the end of the story; then Mr Robinson took out a flat parcel from under his coat. "We waited till you came to open this, Ruth," he said.

With eager hands I tore off the paper and string while Terry watched, and when it was unwrapped, it was so beautiful that we both just gave a little gasp and sat staring at it. We were *so* pleased.

It was a framed picture of a meadow full of clean white sheep all walking one way and nibbling the grass as they went; in front of them walked a Shepherd with a crook, and in his arms lay a little lamb, peacefully asleep.

It was Terry who spoke first.

"Where's he carrying him to?" he asked suddenly, in a worried voice.

"Home, Terry," answered Mr Robinson, with a look on his face that I did not understand then. "Safely through each day until they get home."

"Where's home?" went on Terry.

"It's the place where the Shepherd lives and where we see him face to face," Mr Robinson replied. "Shall I read you something about home, Terry?"

The boy nodded, and Mr Robinson took his New

Testament from his pocket and read in his slow, clear voice about a place where God lived.

"And God shall wipe away all tears from their eyes; and there shall be no more death, neither sorrow nor crying, neither shall there be any more pain."

There was another long silence, then Terry spoke again.

"Cor!" he whispered, thoughtfully, "No more pain! That would be brilliant!" After a minute's thought he added "Can everyone go, or just good people?"

"Why, yes," answered Mr Robinson. "The gate is open for everyone who wishes to go in and who belongs to the Good Shepherd, whether they've been good or bad; you see, the Good Shepherd died to make every one of us fit to go in. There is an old hymn which goes:

'He died that we might be forgiven,
He died to make us good,
That we might go at last to Heaven,
Saved by his precious blood.

There was no other good enough
To pay the price of sin.
He only could unlock the gate
Of Heaven, and let us in.'"

There was another silence, and then Terry whispered, "Tell me some more about them tigers."

And while he lay listening to the tiger story, Terry fell asleep with his hand on his picture, and Mr Robinson and I tiptoed out of the room.

Philip and I went shopping the next Saturday; we bought two daffodil bulbs for Terry, and some fibre to plant them in. We thought we would put them in a bowl on the window-sill so that he could watch the green shoots and the golden flower blossoms next spring. We sat on the floor burying them in the pots, and Terry lay watching us listlessly.

"Funny," said Philip suddenly, "You wouldn't think there was a daffodil hidden down inside this dead-looking old thing, would you?"

"No," I replied, "you wouldn't; there hardly seems room to pack it all inside. I'm going to bury mine near the top, and then it will come up quicker."

"It won't make any difference," said Philip. "It won't come until its proper time, and when that comes, however far under the earth it's lying, it will shoot up at once."

I was about to argue about this when I caught sight of Terry's face. It was even whiter than usual and all twisted up with pain. I wriggled nearer the bed and took hold of his hand.

"Oh, poor Terry!" I cried. "Is it very, very bad? Shall I fetch your mother?"

He shook his head.

"No," he whispered. "She gets so upset when the pain's real bad." Then, with a sob, he added, "Wish I could go to that place where there ain't no more pain."

Philip and I were very upset, for we had never seen Terry like this before; he was such a brave little boy and hardly ever mentioned how much he was suffering.

"I think," said Philip softly, after an uneasy silence, "that we'll ask God to take away your pain

145

and help you go to sleep – like in the Bible when people came to him and he stopped their pains. Kneel down, Ruth, and let's try."

Philip had never prayed aloud before, and the words came very haltingly.

"Dear God – please take away Terry's pain – please make him well soon – please let him go to sleep – Amen."

Then we opened our eyes and looked hopefully at Terry, for we almost expected to see the pain gone immediately from his face. Terry's eyes were open already and fixed on his picture which hung just above his bed.

There were many footsteps up and down the house that night while we lay asleep, for Aunt Margaret and Terry's mother did not go to bed at all, and the doctor arrived just before midnight. But no one heard the feet of the Good Shepherd when he drew near and picked Terry up in his arms.

So Philip's prayer was answered in a way we had never dreamed of. For before the sun had risen again, while the stars were still high in the sky, Terry had left his twisted, suffering body, and all his pain, behind him for ever.

The Shepherd had carried him home.

Chapter Nineteen

Mr Tandy explains

The path to the wood was almost overgrown with yellow bracken and tree branches, but I pressed on because I wanted to get right into the heart of it, far away from everybody, where I could sit and think about the strange things that had happened since Terry died.

I walked a long way – just wandering, kicking at the damp leaves and brushing aside the yellow bracken and trying to forget that we had left Terry alone in the earth. But I could not forget; and when at last I came to a clearing where a great chestnut tree spread out its branches, I lay down on the roots, and resting my head against the trunk I began to cry, and my tears fell thick and fast on the moss.

I was so tired and so miserable that I never heard slow, heavy steps rustling through the leaves, and I jumped when a well-known voice above me spoke to me.

"Why, Ruth, Ruth," said the voice, "what is all this about? You'll catch your death of cold lying there on the ground."

It was Mr Tandy. He stooped down and wrapped his big rough coat about me just as if I had been one of his own stray lambs. Then he sat down on the root, and I snuggled up against him and gave a very big sniff.

I had not seen Mr Tandy for several months because he had left our district to go and work at the Cradley folds. I was very pleased to see him, and very glad to have someone to talk to after my lonely walk. I told him all about what had happened. "I prayed so hard Terry would get better," I said sadly, "but it didn't do any good. God didn't listen, and he died."

"Ruth," replied Mr Tandy slowly, "if you come to me and say 'there's a little lame lamb over there that can't run about' – because the pasture is too steep and the stones sharp – and suppose I came down and picked up that little lamb and carried him in my arms to another pasture where the grass was sweet and the ground easy to run about on, you wouldn't tell me that I hadn't taken any notice of you, would you, now?"

I gazed at him dumbly; I was beginning to understand.

"Ruth," he went on, "the Shepherd took his lamb home, that's all. You've no need to worry."

"But," I cried, my eyes once more filling with tears, "it didn't seem like that at all. They buried Terry in the earth and we left him there, and it seemed so sad and lonely. How can Terry be with the Shepherd when we left him lying in the earth?"

The old man did not answer for a moment, and then he started scraping about with his hands in the leaves as though he was looking for something. His search was rewarded and he held out a shiny brown conker in one hand and an empty seed shell in the other – a withered old thing with green prickles turning brown.

"Now tell me," he said, in his slow, thoughtful voice, "what's going to happen to the conker, and what's going to happen to the covering?"

"Oh," I answered, "the shell will get buried in the leaves and then I suppose it will just wither away. It isn't needed any more; but the conker will grow roots and leaves and turn into a chestnut tree."

"That's right," said Mr Tandy, encouragingly. "You couldn't have said it better. Now tell me this, Ruth; when you see the young chestnut-tree waving its little new leaves in the sunshine next spring, with the birds singing round it, and the rain watering it, you're not going to worry any more for that old case that's crumbled away under the leaves, are you?"

"No," I answered, with my eyes fixed on his face. Once more I thought I understood.

"Well, then," said the old man, joyfully, "you stop worrying for what you laid below the ground – it was just the case. Terry's growing strong in the sunshine."

His kind old eyes lit up with joy as he spoke; he threw down the conker and case and rose stiffly to his feet, because his knees were "full of rheumatics", as he had once told me. Then he took his coat off me and told me to go home.

"For if I don't get along," he said, "I shan't get that gap mended up, and my sheep will be straying out again. Goodbye, Ruth, and God bless you."

I watched him as he moved off into the golden shadows of the wood, and then I stooped down and picked up the conker and its case. Clutching them tightly in my hands, I set off home rather fast, for I was cold and tired and the dusk was falling. When I reached our fields again, the sky was aglow with orange light, and against the sunset stood a little black figure. It was Philip, and he had come to look for me.

I ran to him and slipped my hand into his, and we walked along in comfortable silence. As we climbed the stile, he glanced at my other hand.

"What are you holding so tight?" he asked curiously.

I opened my hand and held out my new treasure.

"It's a conker and its case," I said shyly, "and it's like Terry – Mr Tandy told me so."

"Why?" asked Philip.

"Because," I answered, finding it difficult to explain, "what we put in the earth was like the case; it doesn't matter because Terry didn't need it any more. The inside part that's alive has gone with the Shepherd, so I'm not really sad about it now. Mr Tandy said it was like a lamb being taken to another field where the grass is nicer."

Philip nodded understandingly. "I see," he said, "and I'm glad you're not sad any more."

When we got home, we found that Aunt Margaret had lit a fire in the nursery, and she, Terry's mother, Philip and myself were going to have supper. It was a lovely, picnicky sort of supper with hard-boiled eggs and treacle, ginger-bread, rosy apples and pears, and hot chocolate. I had been for a long walk and Philip had been playing football, so we were both starving! We wriggled nearer the blaze and rubbed our shoulders together to show how much we were enjoying it. Even Terry's mother smiled faintly.

It was when we had eaten all we possibly could that Aunt Margaret, holding out her hands to the blaze, said softly, "Terry's mother and I have been making plans."

"Have you?" we asked, very interested. "Will you tell us?"

"Yes," said my aunt, "because it's a plan that you can both help in – in fact, I shall need your help a great deal. You see, now that little Terry has gone, we want to do something in memory of him. Terry was weak and ill, and we couldn't help him get better – but there are other weak, ill children whom perhaps we could help to get better – and now that I have Terry's mother to help me in the house, and Ruth is getting so handy, I was thinking we'd try to find some of these children and have them here in the holidays. I used to know someone who worked in a prison in London, and I think he could help us. I thought I would write to him and ask him to find two or three little children who needed good food and country air, and invite them here for Christmas. We would give them as lovely a time as possible. Would you like it, Philip and Ruth?"

We thought it was a wonderful idea, and both began to talk at once, eagerly planning what we would do to make it a happy Christmas for them. It was a great relief, for somehow, since Terry died, we had almost felt as though we should not talk about other things, but now we could talk freely and happily about this, for it was all because of Terry and somehow part of Terry.

So we planned about Christmas stockings and Christmas carols and Christmas dinners and Christmas trees, and our cheeks got redder and redder in the firelight and our eyes grew brighter and brighter.

"Auntie," I cried at last, cuddling up against her, "It is a good idea. How did you think of it?"

"Well," replied my aunt, "you are fond of 'Shepherd' verses, so I'll tell you how I thought of it. It was the morning I went to visit Terry for the first time; as I walked through the woods I remembered a verse I had forgotten for years. It was what the Lord Jesus said to one of his disciples just before he went back to Heaven. He said, 'Feed My lambs' – and that's why I wanted Terry to come to us so badly. Then when he died, three mornings ago, I said to myself, 'this lamb doesn't need me any more; but there are plenty of others...'"

She stopped and stared into the fire. I held my hands out to the blaze, and we all sat thinking our own thoughts – sad thoughts about Terry, but all mixed up with happy thoughts about Christmas and the future.

The 'phone bell startled us all, and Aunt Margaret went out to answer it. She was gone some time, and when she returned she was laughing, and her face looked most mysterious.

"Another piece of news," she announced, " and this is the very nicest piece of news we've had for years."

We both stared at her in astonishment. Then suddenly Philip jumped to his feet and made a dash at her.

"I know!" he shouted. "I can guess! Mummy and Daddy are coming home!"

"Yes," she answered, "you've guessed right first time. They will be here in time for Christmas."

Philip's face, flushed with the firelight, was full of joy; but I stayed perfectly still with my hands clasped on my knees. I suddenly felt miserable and all my old fears came back to me. I remembered Aunt Margaret's words of long ago, and how she had said that I should be such a disappointment to my mother, and I didn't want to meet her. She would like Philip better and I would be cross and unhappy and jealous again – and things were just beginning to get comfortable. I turned my head away and looked gloomily at the coal scuttle.

Philip gave me an impatient little shake.

"Aren't you pleased?" he almost screamed. "Why don't you say so?"

I gave a little shrug of my shoulders.

"Yes," I replied, because that was what everyone expected me to say... Then I got up because I wanted to get away from them. "It's bedtime," I said coldly. "Good-night, Aunt Margaret."

But it wasn't really Good-night, for half an hour later Aunt Margaret came softly to where I lay in the dark, and knelt by my bed.

"Ruth," she whispered, and her voice sounded all troubled, "why aren't you glad, like Philip?"

I wriggled uncomfortably and buried my hot face in the pillows; but my aunt did not go away. She waited patiently, and seeing that she really expected an answer, I whispered back.

"You said she wouldn't like me, and I don't suppose she will."

"Oh Ruth!" cried my aunt, "I never said that; I said she would be disappointed when you behaved rudely and selfishly, but that was a long time ago. I know you have been trying hard to be good, and something has certainly made a difference to you. I have felt much happier about you lately, and of course your mother will love you dearly."

I stopped wriggling and lay quite still. I had suddenly stopped feeling shy. "I know what it is," I answered quietly. "It's my picture; it's knowing the Shepherd that's made the difference."

"Yes," agreed Aunt Margaret, "you're right. Your picture, and learning about the Shepherd, has made a tremendous difference to all of us."

Chapter Twenty

A perfect Christmas

It was Christmas evening. We had had such a happy day that I kept having to stop and tell myself that it was all really true.

Mum and Dad had arrived just a fortnight before, and Philip and I had missed school and gone to Liverpool with Uncle Peter to meet the boat. We had been on an escalator, and we had stayed in a hotel where we had chicken and coffee ice-cream for supper, and we had gone up to bed in a lift and the lift man had let Philip work it. Then we had been wakened early, and gone down to the Merseyside in a wet, windy dawn. We had watched the passengers streaming down the gang-way of the great liner, and Uncle Peter had suddenly said in quite a quiet voice, "Here they come," and there were Mum and Dad showing their passports at the barrier.

Philip, absolutely trustful and joyful, had flung himself straight into Dad's arms, and had then turned to Mum and hugged the hat right off her head. But I stood still, because I wanted to be quite sure of everything first; and when Mum ran towards me I looked up into her face and suddenly knew that I had found something I'd been wanting all these years, without knowing it. I was so amazed by it all that I just went on staring up at her, and she didn't hurry me. She waited, looking down at me, until I was ready and held up my arms to kiss her. Then she bent down and put her arms round me and there on the quayside, with the rain falling, and the crowds jostling, and the fog-horns wailing, she told me in a whisper how much she loved me and I made up my mind, then and there, that I was never going to be parted from her again.

Then with one hand in Mum's and one in Dad's, and with Philip prancing round us like an excited puppy, we made our way back to the hotel, had kippers and toast and marmalade for breakfast, and nearly missed the train home.

And now it was Christmas evening and the great moment of the day was approaching. We had opened our stockings, and been to church, and eaten Christmas pudding until we all felt as if we would burst. We had been for a walk on the hills in the afternoon with Dad and Uncle Peter, and had come back as hungry as ever. We had had tea by candlelight, and Dad had cut the cake with his Indian dagger and we had all pulled crackers; but little Minnie, one of the London children, didn't like the bangs and had been carried out screaming and fed with chocolate biscuits in the kitchen by

Terry's mother, whom she adored. Now Auntie was saying, "Run away for five minutes, children," and Mum was saying, "Go into the kitchen and see how Minnie is getting on." Philip pinched us all in turns and said, "Come on everybody, now's our chance."

So when the lounge door was safely shut on the grown-ups, we slipped on our coats and tiptoed out of the front door. The world was quite silent and the starlight lay silver on the snow. Philip looked hard at us and hummed the note, and then we all threw back our heads and started singing the carol we had learned to sing to the grown-ups.

While I was singing, I kept thinking that the Baby Jesus was now my shepherd, who was going to look after me day and night, and carry me home some day to where Terry was. I knew that I was perfectly safe for ever and ever.

When the carol was over, Alfie hammered excitedly on the door. It was flung open, and there in the hall, under the mistletoe and holly, were Mum and Auntie in paper hats and Dad and Uncle pretending they didn't know it was us, and Terry's mother with tears in her eyes and little Minnie clasped tightly in her arms. We flung ourselves wildly upon them.

"Did you like it?" we shouted. "Did you really think it wasn't us?"

We tumbled inside, took off our coats and went to gather round the Christmas tree, which we had dug up from the Cowleigh woods. It was now beautifully decorated – the candles were alight and shed a rosy glow over the room.

It was so pretty that we stopped shouting, and sat

down quietly, cross-legged on the floor, while Dad started giving out the presents. The little Londoners were thrilled with their gifts and soon it was our turn. Dad took a square parcel from the pile at the bottom of the tree and handed it to Philip.

"Open it carefully, Phil!" he warned. "It's very fragile."

Philip annoyed me by taking a long time over the unwrapping, but he always liked to make his pleasures last as long as possible. However, at last it came to light, and Philip made a funny noise in his throat like something trying not to explode. It was a black Kodak camera, just like the one we had so often gazed at in the windows of the chemist's shop.

"Philip!" I squealed, "you've got it!" Then I stopped short, for of course it was my turn now. Dad had chosen a flat, hard parcel and was holding it out to me.

Everyone crowded round to watch as I, unlike Philip, tore the wrappings off as quickly as possible and gave a little gasp of delight and went pink all over.

It was my own picture, but not a crumpled, torn postcard one. It was a big, beautiful copy in a carved wooden frame for me to hang over my bed and keep for ever. In fact, it was just like the one in Mr Robinson's study.

The grown-ups opened their presents after that, and seemed as pleased as we were; they were mostly home-made things and we were very proud of them; wooden book-ends for Uncle Peter, a purse for Aunt Margaret, a blotter for Dad and a hot-water bottle cover for Mum. Terry's mother was presented with a highly-coloured embroidered handkerchief case, which she admired very much indeed. Of course, there were other presents, too, but these were the main ones; and by the time everyone had opened everything Minnie was found to be fast asleep in Terry's mother's arms and Lizzie in her new green dress was nodding against the wall. So they were carried off and tucked in.

Philip and I helped clear up, and then Philip and Dad sat down on the sofa and looked at the bird book together for about the tenth time. But it was different now, because the camera lay in Philip's lap and they were planning the photos.

I wandered off by myself with my picture in my arms, and climbed the stairs. I wanted to curl up behind the curtain on the landing window-sill and look out at the Christmas stars and snow, and listen to the bells that were ringing from the church near by. But when I reached my hiding place, I found that Mum had got there first, and that was even better than being alone, so I climbed onto her lap and held up my picture because I wanted us to look at it together.

"Isn't it beautiful?" I asked.

"Yes," replied Mum, "but what made you love it so specially, Ruth? Tell me about it."

So I told her, rather shyly, and she listened, looking out over the snow, until I had finished.

"And it's not only me," I ended up. "He found me first, but after that he found Philip and Terry's mother, and he found Terry, too, and carried him right home; and, Mummy, sometimes I wonder if he found Aunt Margaret, too. At least, I think she had forgotten about him a bit and when she saw the picture it reminded her of him again."

"Yes, I think it did," answered Mum, "and do you know, Ruth, I also want to learn so much about him. Sometimes, far away in India, I used to pray that somehow you would get to know about him, but I never felt I knew enough to teach you myself."

I looked up quickly.

"Did you really?" I exclaimed. "Then I suppose that's why it all happened – you sort of sent him to us. I'm glad it's like that, because it makes it even nicer than it was before."

I laid my head against her shoulder, and we sat quietly looking out. I think I nearly fell asleep, and in a half-dreaming way I saw us all found, and following through the green fields in Terry's picture; Mum and Dad, Auntie and Uncle; Mr and Mrs Robinson and the twins, their tiny feet stumbling through the daisies; old Mr Tandy with his flock behind him; Terry's mother; Philip and me; Alfie and Lizzie and Minnie – because I had promised to tell them all about my picture in the morning; and, in front of us all, the Good Shepherd with the wounded hands leading us on to a Land far away where Terry was, perfectly strong and happy.